Smooth Intentions 2

Kimberly Stewart

Acknowledgement

I truly thank all of my true friends and fans of my work. I love coming out with new ideas. It has been a wonderful experience to write my books. It has always been my dream to become an author. Your love and support means a lot to me. A lot of people said I don't have what it takes to be an author. I choose to prove them wrong, you can be anyone you want to be with faith and the uplifting of good love from heaven above.

It has been an amazing experience to be recognized and told by people how much they love my books. My husband and my kids are the people that have helped me push forward and I'm thankful for their support all the way. When you read my books you will be very excited to see what is going to happen next. My books will have you wanting more to the very end.

I'm very honored to provide books on a low income budget for people to enjoy. I plan to write books in every gene of fiction - YA, romance, children's books and nonfiction too.

I hope you enjoy!! Love is life and Life is love!

Kimberly Stewart

Dedication

This book is dedicated to my friends and loved ones.

Table of Contents

Acknowledgement 2

Dedication 3

Chapter one 6

Chapter two 46

Chapter three 62

Chapter four 78

Chapter five 112

Chapter six 121

Smooth Intentions 2

ISBN 978-069-250-4062

Printed in USA by Dreamgirl Publishing, LL

Chapter One

Skylar Clark was now the newest face of Clark Enterprises. She was honored that her grandfather gave her the opportunity to run Clark Enterprises. Skylar and her father Monty kept Clark Enterprises successful as it has always been. In Skylar's heart she was missing her grandfather and all she could think about was getting revenge against Mr. Bowler. Skylar tried to track down Mr. Bowler with a private eye across America. There was no trace of him. It was as if he had vanished. Skylar came to the conclusion that he was no longer in America. Mr. Bowler was in another country hoping not to be found. She made a promise to herself that it wasn't over until he was found, and she would avenge her grandfather's death. She remembered the anonymous man at her grandfather's funeral, dressed in black tossing up a gold coin before he disappeared. She was thinking to herself was it really real or was that a spirit sent by a loved one to protect the family? Skylar was at her desk when the phone rang.

"Uncle Kenny, how are you?"

"I'm so happy for you, how does it feel to be the newest face of Clark's Enterprises?" said Kenny.

"It's a lot of work, but dad and the rest of the employees are helping to make it a huge success." said Skylar. "What have you been doing?"

"I got a job working with the newspaper New World Times." said Kenny.

"I've heard about them, they travel around the world reporting the news from different countries. That's so cool." said Skylar.

"It's alright; it pays pretty well." said Kenny.

"Where is Monty?" Asked Kenny

"He is in his office; do you want me to get him?" asked Skylar.

"No, just tell my brother that I love him, and I'm doing well." said Kenny.

"I will Uncle Kenny, love you." said Skylar.

"Love you too Skylar." said Kenny.

They said goodbye and hung up, Skylar knew that Kenny was the cause of the loss of her grandfather, but Mr. Bowler was already ready to steal the company away from the Clark's family. She knew more than anything, her grandfather didn't want her to turn her back on Kenny. She made a promise to herself, no matter what she will revenge his death. As she was sitting in her office, she saw a picture of her grandfather; she grabbed the picture and felt tears streaming down her face. Monty stopped by her office.

"Skylar what's wrong? Are you ok?" said Monty.

"I'm ok dad." said Skylar.

Monty looked at her holding the picture of his father and gave her a hug.

"It's going to be ok." said Monty.

"Dad, I'm fine. I have to be strong." said Skylar.

"We all have to be strong."

"Dad, by the way Kenny called." said Skylar.

"Why didn't you tell me?" asked Monty.

"You were busy in your office, he told me to tell you that he loves you." said Skylar.

"So how is he doing?" said Monty.

"Kenny is doing extremely well. He works for New world Times." said Skylar.

"New World Times?" asked Monty.

"He travels around the world, writing about news from different parts of the world." said Skylar.

"I'm so proud of him." said Monty.

"Dad, how about we finish up here and get something to eat." said Skylar.

"Sounds like a good idea." said Monty.

They had a nice time together just father and daughter. When they got to the mansion they saw there was a strange car in the yard. Wondering who it could be, as they stepped into the mansion, Ms. Rosa told Skylar she had a surprise for her.

Ms. Rosa yelled out you can come out now! It was Rico, her friend from high school who, after graduation left to join the Army. Skylar was shocked, she ran to him and gave him a big hug.

"Why are you here?" said Skylar.

"The army sent all the soldiers home to see our family and friends before we go overseas for war." said Rico.

"So how long are you going to be here?" said Skylar.

"For just a couple of days. So I had to come see you." said Rico.

"I'm so happy to see you." said Skylar.

Ms. Rosa and Monty left the room, so those two could be alone. They sat down together in the living room, he grabbed her hands. "I'm so sorry about your grandfather, I'm sorry I couldn't be there to support you" said Rico.

"That's ok." said Skylar.

"Another thing, I have always wanted to tell you Skylar Clark, something that I have kept inside, I've wanted to tell you that I love you. I've wanted to tell you since high school but there is something about feeling scared, of a girl that knows martial arts."

Skylar just laughed.

"You're the most beautiful young woman I have ever seen." said Rico.

"Thanks Rico that means a lot to me. I have something to tell you also. I love you too." said Skylar.

"I would love to take you to dinner tomorrow." said Rico.

"I would like that." said Skylar.

He gave her a kiss and told her he would see her tomorrow. She looked out the door waving and he was waving back. Skylar went upstairs to her room to figure out the perfect outfit to wear. Monty and Ms. Rosa had a discussion about Rico.

"I think Skylar's heart is about to be broken." said Monty.

"They're in love." said Ms. Rosa

"He's leaving to go with the army back overseas, it might be love and goodbye. She lost her grandfather and that still affects her." said Monty.

"What you have to understand is she not that same little girl anymore. She's a grown woman and she can make decisions on her own." said Ms. Rosa

"I know that but Skylar has been through a lot." said Monty.

"Skylar knows how to defend herself, she a smart girl. She had two good trainers who have taught her well. Before anyone is going to take her down she's taking them down first." said Ms. Rosa.

"Your right about that. I guess I have to learn to let her go. But I just don't trust Rico." said Monty.

"Monty you're her father and fathers are going to be overprotective of their daughters, and I know that Skylar will be just fine, she's smiling for a change." said Ms. Rosa

"Your right Ms. Rosa, what would I do without you?" wondered Monty.

"I don't know." laughed Ms. Rosa.

"I'm going to bed." said Monty. "Goodnight Ms. Rosa."

"Goodnight Monty." said Ms. Rosa.

***

The next day, Skylar was so excited about her day with Rico. She wore her red dress and diamond earrings with her red high heels and went to the hairdresser to get her hair and nails done. A lady name Carol Lane owned Beautiful Essence Beauty Salon. She heard she was the best in town. She made the most amazing styles and won competitions. People loved the beautiful styles she creates. Skylar walked into the beauty salon.

"Hi, how can I help you?" said Carol.

"I'm Skylar Clark, I have appointment."

"The Skylar Clark that owns Clark Enterprises? asked Carol.

"The one and only." said Skylar.

"It's a pleasure to meet you." said Carol.

Everyone in the beauty salon heard her name and looked.

"Have a seat in my chair." said Carol.

Skylar went over to the chair to have a seat.

"Is there a certain style you're looking for?" said Carol Lane.

"I'm going on a date, so I need you to work your magic and make me look beautiful." said Skylar.

"Do you want your nails done too?" said Carol.

"Yes." said Skylar

"Ok, let's get ready" said Carol and both ladies high fived each other.

A little later a lady came into the beauty salon very angry. The reception asked her if she was okay.

"You can help me, by getting Carol Lane out here." said the angry woman.

"I'm sorry, but Ms. Lane is busy right now." the receptionist explained.

The woman yelled "I'm not leaving until I see her." Carol came out. "What seems to be the problem?" she asked.

"The problem is that I'm unhappy with my hair." said the angry woman.

"Why?" said Carol

"Why? Because I wanted it dyed just like in the magazine I was looking at." said the angry woman.

"I tried to tell you that having a relaxer and a permanent hair color would be hard on your hair." said Carol.

"I don't care! I want what I asked for." said the angry woman.

Carol advised the woman that it would jeopardize her business and she cares about the health of her hair. As Carol was talking, the reception called the police. The police were just around the corner, and so they came into the beauty salon.

The reception said "That's her, she threatened us and she wouldn't leave."

"Is that right? Ms. Lane?" the policeman enquired.

"Yes." said Carol.

The policeman placed handcuffs on the lady, Skylar approached the policeman and asked to speak to the woman.

"I want to tell you, you are a beautiful woman, just as you are" said Skylar. "What made you behave this way?"

"My husband left me for another woman." said the angry woman.

"What your name?" asked Skylar.

"Jennifer Sage" the woman replied. "I tried to be the best wife I could be but it wasn't enough." she explained. "She's a model, I could never compete with that."

"Just hold on and be strong" said Skylar. "God is always there when you need him. Do you have the house?" said Skylar.

"Yes and the children" said Jennifer.

"I'll help you get in contact with a good lawyer" said Skylar. "Everything that he has belongs to you and don't worry about the expenses, everything is on me." said Skylar.

Skylar gave her a card, and a hug.

Skylar, told the policeman to un-cuff her and that everything was alright, the policeman left.

She told Skylar thank you so much, the woman was smiling and left happy.

"Thank you, so much for saving my business." said Carol.

"You're welcome! Now time to make me beautiful." said Skylar.

Skylar went to sit in the beauty chair and Carol began doing her hair. Later, Carol was through with the hair and her nails.

Carol asked Skylar if she was ready to see. She rolled her chair around, Skylar couldn't believe her eyes. Her hair was full of elegant curls and her red nails were studded with diamonds. She couldn't believe her eyes.

"Oh, my god! It's beautiful." said Skylar.

"Indeed it is." said Carol.

Everyone looked and admired the wonderful job Carol had done. Skylar paid Carol with her MasterCard and thanked her for making her look so wonderful. Carol wished her luck for her date.

***

Skylar left the beauty salon and went back to the mansion. As Skylar came through the door everyone was shocked. Ms. Rosa and Bertha Ann greeted her and told her how beautiful she was.

"Bertha Ann I'm so happy to see you." said Skylar.

"Oh, you're my family. I love you like you are my own daughter." said Bertha Ann.

Bertha Ann had her own bakery shop, her bakery was a success and yet she would come and work for the Clark's family sometimes.

I'd love to chat, but I have a date that I don't want to miss." said Skylar.

"Ok." said Bertha Ann and Ms. Rosa

Skylar got dressed, her date Rico was on his way. After a while, Rico came with flowers and in his army uniform. Rosa let him in and offered him a seat.

Skylar came down the stairs; she was glowing, like an angel. As she was coming down the stairs Rico greeted her and told her she was beautiful. He gave her flowers and a kiss. Skylar smiled and asked him if was ready to go.

"Yes I'm ready." said Rico.

"Enjoy yourselves." said Ms. Rosa and Bertha Ann.

Rico opened the car door for her as she got in. He drove off and they were on their way to a nice fancy restaurant called Angelou's Finest. As they pulled up to the door, the valet parked Rico's car.

As they got in the waiter had them seated. Skylar look all around it was so pretty, there was a little foundation which had a fish aquarium, beautiful shining chandeliers and elegant tables.

"This is a beautiful restaurant." said Skylar.

I wanted to take you to somewhere special? said Rico. He caressed her face with his hand and gave her a kiss. "I wanted a romantic evening with you."

"Aww! That's so sweet Rico." said Skylar.

The waiter approached them and asked them if they would like a drink.

"I would like a bottle of your most expensive champagne." said Rico.

"Ok, sir." said the waiter.

"What would you like from the menu?" asked the waiter.

Rico asked Skylar if there was anything she liked.

Skylar looked, and told the waiter she would like the lobster. Rico ordered the same. The waiter hurried on off.

"You're sure you can afford this?" asked Skylar.

"I'm sure." said Rico.

"Rico this is a lot for our first date." said Skylar.

"Skylar, I always loved you but I just couldn't say it before." said Rico.

"Rico, I have always loved you too." said Skylar.

"I know that you have all that you ever need, you own a billion dollar company." said Rico.

"Rico, I like you for who you are no amount of money is worth that." said Skylar.

The waiter came back with the champagne and poured it into the champagne glasses for the both of them. And then served them their dinner. As they ate, laughed and drank champagne they enjoyed their time with each other.

Rico and Skylar spend the night at Rico's place.

***

The next morning Skylar woke up to the aroma of eggs, bacon and coffee. Rico had cooked breakfast for her. Rico told her to have a seat, as he brought breakfast to the table. Skylar sat down and ate her breakfast, and then Rico's phone rang. It was the army telling him he needed to leave as soon as possible, in one hour.

Rico asked them was there any way he could stay a little while longer. They told him he couldn't. They ate quickly and soon it was time for Rico to take the plane. Skylar started to cry, it was too soon for him to leave.

Rico said "Don't cry I promise I will come back to you." He gave her a hug and a kiss, reached for his jacket which had his dog tags with his name and gave them to her. "I want you to have them."

Skylar quickly put them on her neck. It was heartbreaking for him to leave Skylar. He got his army bag and told Skylar to drive back safely. Skylar was standing looking as he was getting on the plane, her hair was blowing in the wind, he threw his hand up and waved goodbye. She watched the plane take off. As she was standing there as the wind was blowing she felt a cold chill and all of a sudden heard her grandfather voice *"You shouldn't let him go..."* She quickly got into the car and the wind stopped. Skylar quickly went back to the mansion.

***

Rico flew on the plane back to the army base, as he got back to the base, he was reunited with the other soldiers. One soldier was always by himself and was always acting suspicious like he had something to hide. The other soldiers felt Rico just didn't like him, because he was the sergeant's favorite. Rico felt that he wasn't all he seemed to be.

The sergeant got everyone together and had a meeting about some strange things that had been happening at the army base. Shipments of the army guns were disappearing, and he thought there was a traitor in the army. The sergeant told everyone to keep a sharp eye out.

The main person the sergeant trusted was Marcus Stamps, but Rico felt in his gut that it was he who was responsible. Marcus helped out with the gun shipments and several of the soldiers were caught in gunfire. Marcus was not hurt, the other soldiers thought that he was lucky. Rico knew it wasn't luck and wished the others could believe it too.

***

Skylar was at the mansion talking to her father about how Rico had to go back to the army.

18

"Dad I wish he didn't have to go." said Skylar.

"I know Skylar, but when the army calls he has to go." said Monty.

Tears were falling from her eyes, Ms. Rosa saw her crying and gave her tissues to wipe her tears. Ms. Rosa told her that long distance relationships were never easy but their love for each other would keep their bond strong.

"I think I'll go to the old warehouse to do some gun and martial arts training." said Skylar.

"Are you sure you're alright?" said Monty.

"Yes dad." said Skylar.

What made Skylar better was doing her training. To her it made her strong enough to conquer anything.

***

The soldiers were glad to be back together and decided to go out for drinks, a guy's night out. Rico decided he would stay and investigate Marcus things to see what he was hiding and if his suspicions were right. As everyone was leaving they noticed Rico hanging behind.

"Have a good time! I'll stay here." said Rico

"Ok." said Frank.

Rico watched as everyone left and made sure the coast was clear. He looked around Marcus' bunk but there was nothing, then around the side he saw a box. He opened the box. It contained a letter with a list of weapons and addresses to ship the weapons to along with a picture. The picture was shocking. It was a group of guys dressed in black and it had him and Mr. Bowler shaking hands. Rico was shocked by it.

Mr. Bowler was still alive. Rico knew Skylar had been searching for Mr. Bowler and wanted to tell her, but Rico didn't know what else to suspect. He didn't want Skylar to get hurt. Rico knew that Skylar would take the first flight there. He remember when he had to leave her to go back to the army it was hard looking back waving back at her. By telling her it could be the last time he would see her.

Rico didn't know if Marcus was the only one in the army that was involved. He decided he would keep what he found a secret. He would continue to keep his eyes open around the army.

***

Skylar was at Killermike's warehouse, she kept it after Killermike died so she could train. Killermike was her friend and not just her trainer. Killermike's leather coat was sitting on the chair. Skylar looked at it as memories flashed in her mind of her moments with Killermike. A tear came from Skylar eyes. She was there before he got shot multiple shots trying to save her. She felt if it wasn't for Killermike and Kiana's teaching and training she wouldn't be who she was today.

Skylar went over to the guns and loaded them, ready to do her training. Skylar combined her gun training and martial arts training. But the training they taught her, she wanted it to be better. She trained very hard with the guns and kicks and spins and fired at the figures for her training. After she was done with her training she took a drink of Killermike's whiskey and had a seat.

Skylar had started thinking about how much she missed them, looking at the photo of her and Killermike. Skylar wanted to put flowers on Killermike and Kiana's graves. Skylar grabbed Killermike's leather coat and put it on before leaving. She grabbed some flowers from the side of the warehouse to put on the graves. Skylar drove to the graveyard where Killermike and Kiana were buried.

When she arrived it looked like someone or somebody had desecrated the graves. Skylar dropped to her knees saddened and disgusted at the fact that someone could do something like this.

Skylar took out her cell phone and called the chief of police. The chief of police told her he was on his way. Skylar saw where it looked like someone had climb out of their graves, and there was no bodies. All that Skylar could think about was this could be the work of Mr. Bowler. Skylar searched around looking to see if there was any evidence that might point to who did this.

Skylar found what seemed like a track, tire tracks of a large vehicle had been recently here. Maybe uploading Killermike and Kiana bodies, it was a mystery why they would want their bodies.

Later the chief of police arrived and the rest of the squad arrived. Checking around for evidence of who could do this. They found out the graves had no bodies; they saw the tire tracks and took pictures. The chief asked Skylar if she was okay.

"Yes, I'm fine, I just want you to find out who did this to my friends, I won't rest until their bodies are found." said Skylar.

"Don't worry Skylar." said the chief of police. "We will find out, who did this."

Skylar got back to the mansion and told her father what was going on.

Monty gave her a hug as she cried "Dad why?"

"Skylar there are some cruel people in this world, who don't care about anyone." said Monty.

"Dad, my guess is Mr. Bowler has something to do with this." said Skylar.

"I think so too." said Monty.

"Dad, I want to find out why he did this?" said Skylar.

"Mr. Bowler is still after Clark Enterprises." said Monty. "Mr. Bowler will try anything to rattle you and taking them was one way to do it."

"Dad, I will find him and I will finish him even if it's the last thing I do." said Skylar.

"I heard that he might be overseas, but still he has goons here working for him." said Monty.

Later, Skylar went to visit Kiana's family. She already called them and informed them about the situation. Kiana's family was very upset about the fact that someone had desecrated their daughter's grave and that the body was missing. The family was wondering who would do something so terrible. Skylar rang the doorbell, a lady answer the door.

"Is this Mr. & Mrs. Lei?" asked Skylar

"Yes, it is." said Mrs. Lei

"I'm Skylar Clark one of Kiana's Students." said Skylar.

"Oh, yes." said Mr. Lei. "Come on in, come on in. You were the little girl Kiana trained. Have a seat. Would you like some tea?"

"Yes, please." said Skylar.

As Mrs. Lei went to get the tea, Skylar looked around the room full of pictures of Lei's family. The family was all involved in Kajukenbo mixed martial arts; there were pictures of them in battle, and newspaper article clippings about the Lei's family. Ms. Lei came back into the room with Skylar's tea.

"I see you are amazed at our family, we have been in mixed martial arts for generations." said Mr. Lei.

"Mr. Lei I've learnt a lot from Kiana. She wasn't just a teacher to me, she was a friend." said Skylar.

"I'm very sorry for your loss" said Skylar. "I will avenge her death."

"My daughter has taught you well, you took on the mob and lived through it." said Mr. Lei. "Even though Kiana has trained you well, remember your inner soul is what will guide you through the battles. Skylar you have the heart of a lion and the soul of the eagle flying to great heights. I am also sorry for your loss of your grandfather."

"Skylar you have inherited a billion dollar company, now that you own it, they will come after you." said Mr. Lei.

"I'll be waiting for them." said Skylar.

"Skylar my daughter is always here in spirit." said Mr. Lei.

He threw out his arms. "Skylar welcome to our family." said Mr. Lei.

Skylar got back into the car and headed home. At the mansion, the phone rang. Monty answered. It was Kenny.

"Hey brother, what's happening?" asked Kenny

"Kenny, how are you doing?" asked Monty.

"I'm doing fine." said Kenny "How is everyone? Where is Skylar?"

"Skylar went to meet the Lei family, Kiana and Killermike's bodies are missing." said Monty

"What happened?" Kenny enquired.

"That's what we're trying to figure out." said Monty.

"If I know Skylar she's going to get to the bottom of things." said Kenny.

"You know it." said Monty.

"I call to let you know what happens. I'll be leaving… I'm going overseas." said Kenny.

"Now, Kenny please don't get into any trouble while you're away." Monty joked. "I know you're a journalist and finding stories is your job!"

"Don't worry brother, I'll be fine." said Kenny. "I'll call to let you know I'm ok."

"So what's the story you're going after?" asked Monty.

"The army is going to war overseas." said Kenny. "Also there are rumors going around that the army has a traitor inside selling their weapons illegally. So New World Times are sending me overseas to find out what's going on."

"Kenny, are you sure about this profession?" said Monty.

"I love it. I finally found what I've been dreaming of, to see the world." said Kenny. "For years, I stayed at the mansion… I had hate towards you, that you were dad's favorite. But I realized I was wrong I shouldn't have treated you that way. You're my brother."

"Thanks Kenny." said Monty.

"Well I think I have to get ready to board this flight." said Kenny. "Tell Skylar where I am."

"I will." said Monty.

At Eagles Land Airport, you could hear the intercom announcing that flight 9862 was boarding. There was someone boarding the fight with Kenny. The photographer with the New World Times named Scott Bistol. Kenny was walking in the airport with dark shades like he was a big time celebrity like Jay-z.

Scott carried their bags, the bags were extra heavy and Scott struggled getting them on board. Finally, they got on the plane with everything, and flight 9862 took off. Kenny was enjoying first class with expensive wine! The steward on the plane asked Scott if he wanted anything, Scott only asked for water.

Kenny suggested he have some wine but Scott refused. "I like to be professional when I'm on a business trip." Scott explained.

"I think you can be professional and drink too! We have a long flight man live it up." said Kenny.

Scott reached into his pocket and grabbed his earplugs connecting it to his mp3 player to not hear a word Kenny was saying. This was going to be a long flight.

***

Skylar came back home.

"Hi dad how have you been?" asked Skylar.

"Kind of worried." Monty admitted.

"Why?" asked Skylar

"Well it seems like your uncle Kenny is going to be conducting a story." said Monty.

"That's his job, dad." said Skylar.

"Skylar you don't know what he is doing a story on. There are things going on in the army, there is a traitor in the army stealing weapons." said Monty. "If Kenny goes after this story he's going to get a lot more than he bargained for."

"So you mean to tell me that Kenny is going to the army where Rico is? Skylar asked. "I just hope they both get home safely. If I sense any trouble I'm going out there."

"Skylar you have a business to run, how are you going to be able to save them if they're in trouble?" Monty asked.

"Dad, you can take charge of the company, if anything were to happen" said Skylar.

"Skylar absolutely not! "If anything was to happen to you I would never forgive myself. You are all I have" said Monty.

"Dad, I'm not a little girl anymore, I have killed members of the mob." Skylar reminded him. "I can take care of myself."

"If you go please I beg of you take as many people as possible." said Monty.

"Ok, dad." said Skylar.

"It's a battle, one person cannot handle it all alone." said Monty.

"Dad, where is Ms. Rosa?" Skylar asked.

"She's right outside." said Monty.

Skylar went outside to talk to Ms. Rosa.

"What brings you out here?" Ms. Rosa wondered.

"I wanted to talk to you." said Skylar

"Well you know my heart is always open." said Ms. Rosa.

"It's just life, I want things to be better for my family and I don't want to give up the fight, It's a battle that continues and I know as long as we are wealthy, the people we love will be in danger." said Skylar.

"Skylar, what you have to realize is that you have to keep faith, honey! Everything happens for a reason, god gave you gift, you use it to protect the ones you love." said Ms. Rosa.

Ms. Rosa put her hands on Skylar's face. "My child, don't you ever give up! Life is hard but we have to be strong."

Skylar hugged her and thanked her for her kindness.

***

At the army base, Rico was sitting looking at a picture of Skylar. Hoping and praying that nothing happened to Skylar. He was missing her. Marcus saw Rico and smiled

"What seems to be the problem? Rico accidental dropped the picture and said "It's none of your concern."

The picture was on the floor and Marcus glanced at it. Marcus had seen a picture of her in Mr. Bowler's office, and remembered Mr. Bowler saying that she killed his goons, she wasn't going rest till he was dead too.

"Rico, I have the feeling that you don't like me?" Marcus asked while smiling.

"I don't like you." said Rico.

"You dropped something." said Marcus.

"I know. You just need to get away from me." said Rico.

Marcus just wanted to take a cheap shot at Rico, he walked by him and told him to have a nice day.

After walking out of the room, Marcus made a call. "Mr. Bowler I think we have problem."

"What is it?" Mr. Bowler snapped.

"It's that cat here named Rico, he has a picture of that woman you said killed your goons." said Marcus.

"Tell me, what does she look like?" asked Mr. Bowler

"She has black curly hair, a gorgeous black woman, just like the photo boss." said Marcus.

"That's Skylar." said Mr. Bowler. "So the young man there is her boyfriend?" asked Mr. Bowler.

"Yeah, boss and I think he knows about me!" said Marcus

"Marcus, if he gets in your way eliminate him, as soon as possible." said Mr. Bowler. "I will not allow anyone to jeopardize my shipments. In fact, we should kill two birds with one stone."

"What do you mean Mr. Bowler?" said Marcus.

"If he gets in your way, you can use him as bait, to draw out his girlfriend Skylar, she now owns Clark Enterprises, and I would do anything to have that company. It's worth billions of dollars and so is she." said Mr. Bowler.

"Mr. Bowler are you sure about this? said Marcus. "She has killed a lot of goons."

"Now, that I have you and some of the men from the army, she has no chance." said Mr. Bowler. "And when we capture the two of them I will enjoy killing them both. I'll make her sign the contract to turn over Clark Enterprises to me in return for releasing her. I'm evil to the core, I don't keep promises. Marcus, keep an eye on him, and don't slip up. I'll be in touch"

"Yes, will do" said Marcus.

Marcus got off the cell phone while all the soldiers lined up in single file .The sergeant came to talk about the great battle they would encounter. They stood straight as he spoke.

"Who are we?" yelled the sergeant.

"Soldiers." they replied.

"What kind of soldiers?" said the sergeant.

"Soldiers of the United States army, sir." yelled the soldiers.

"As you go to battle, you are not to turn on each other. You are all family of the United States army." said the sergeant. "Give me 150 push-ups."

After that they did extensive training, climbing, running and also gun training shooting an M-16 rifle and an M-4 carbine, disassembling, cleaning and reassembling the weapons. Marcus and Rico gave each other an evil look but did their training as the sergeant instructed.

As the day turned into night, all of the soldiers were sound asleep. All Rico could think about was Skylar. He went into the office to use the phone to call Skylar.

"Rico, Is it you?" said Skylar.

"Yes, it's me." said Rico. "I had to call you and tell you that I miss you."

"I miss you too. Rico, strange things have been happening here." said Skylar.

"Strange things like what?" said Rico

"Killermike and Kiana's graves were desecrated, their bodies are missing and I think Mr. Bowler has something to do with it." said Skylar.

"Why do you say that?" asked Rico.

"I know Mr. Bowler, he'll do anything to get to me." said Skylar.

"Skylar, I love you dearly, but I don't want you to fight Mr. Bowler without any help." said Rico.

"Funny, that the same thing, my dad said." said Skylar.

"Where's Monty?" said Rico.

"He's right here." said Skylar.

"Dad, Rico wants to talk to you." said Skylar.

"It's good to hear from you Rico." said Monty

"I have something to tell you, it's about the army and the things they have going on here." said Rico

"I know they're stealing army weapons." said Monty.

"Yeah, how did you hear about it?" said Rico.

"Actually! Kenny told me." said Monty.

"Kenny!" said Rico

"Kenny is flying there to the army base to do an article about the stolen weapons." said Monty.

"I wish I knew Kenny was on the way." said Rico. "He could be walking into big trouble."

"Rico, what's going on?" said Monty.

"Some of the soldiers here are involved with the mob." said Rico.

"What mob?" said Monty.

"Mr. Bowler is alive" Said Rico. "He has soldiers working for him, stealing the weapons."

"The last thing I wanted to hear was that he's involved, if Kenny gets there give me a call. If he's in any trouble…" said Monty.

"I'll do my best to keep him out of it if I can." said Rico.

"What we can't do is let Skylar know." said Monty.

"I agree." said Rico.

"There are some things that may lead her in that direction." said Monty. "When the time is right I'll tell her what she needs to know."

"Monty what other things are going on?" Said Rico.

"I'm not sure, but I have a feeling that there is more to it." said Monty. "Make sure you don't mention Mr. Bowler to her."

"Yes sir." said Rico. Rico noticed a shadow by the door while he was on the phone but when he looked for a second time the shadow had disappeared.

"Is everything ok?" Monty asked.

"Yes." Rico replied. "Put Skylar on the phone."

"Skylar I love you, I guess I should go back before someone realizes that I'm on the phone." said Rico.

"I love you, talk to you later, bye." said Rico

"Love you too." said Skylar.

Rico didn't know that there was someone at the door listening to him. It was Marcus. He quickly got back in the room, with the other soldiers that were sleep. Rico went back to his army bed.

***

Skylar was up the next day, ready to go to work at Clark Enterprises. They had a meeting about the stocks. During the meeting she felt her phone vibrate.

Hi, Skylar this is Josh. Meet me downstairs.

Skylar excused herself and went down to the lobby.

"Wow it's Skylar Clark with a suit, you look like a professional business woman." Said Josh.

"Well thank you." said Skylar

"Skylar I heard about what happened to Kiana and Killermike's graves. I think Mr. Bowler is involved." Said Josh.

"I do too!" said Skylar.

"I'm going to get to bottom of it. Skylar, you don't know who you are going up against." said Josh. "I think you'll need back-up."

"Who do you think I should get?" said Skylar.

"What about me and I have a guy name Levi Griffen. He's a big guy." Josh showed her a picture of him, Levi was a black man with muscles who was very strong and who could pack a punch and shoot in a blink of an eye. Skylar agreed they were perfect for the job.

Skylar went back to her meeting, after the meeting was over, she asked her father if he was going home. Monty told her he was staying to catch up with paperwork. So Skylar drove back home alone.

At home she decided to change into her street fighting gear. She put on Killermike's leather coat and texted Josh, asking him to meet her Fat Louie's place.

When Skylar got to Fat Louie's, Josh was sitting at the bar with Levi drinking a beer, Josh waved at Skylar. She wondered how they had gotten there so fast.

"Didn't take long with his driving." said Levi.

"So what I want to know is what you think it's going to take to find Mr. Bowler." said Skylar.

"It's going to take weapons." said Josh. "Even though you killed his goons last time doesn't mean he doesn't have a larger, bigger and better mob this time. Mr. Bowler did a lot to people, you are not the only one that wants revenge."

"Levi worked for Mr. Bowler, many years ago. Levi was always following Mr. Bowler's orders but Mr. Bowler was killing innocent people for his own amusement. This was where Levi drew the line. Levi told Mr. Bowler, that he didn't want to work for him anymore." said Josh.

"Did he ever know Killermike?" Said Skylar.

"No." Josh replied.

"He wasn't working for Mr. Bowler when it happened." said Josh.

"So what happen after he stopped working for Mr. Bowler?" Skylar asked.

"Mr. Bowler killed everyone Levi loved." Said Josh.

As Levi was listening to Josh describing his story he downed several shots of liquor hoping it would help him cope.

Skylar asked the bartender to give her a shot of liquor. She drank it down really fast.

"I know how you feel." said Skylar. "My family means the world to me. I will get my revenge."

"We both will." said Levi while shaking her hand.

"What we have to do is come up with a plan." said Josh. "We need to find where Mr. Bowler is hiding out."

"What about his old neighborhood?" said Levi.

"Yes! We should check it out." said Josh. "Meanwhile, I'll call my friends from the CIA to see what they can find out."

"We will find him." said Skylar.

"We are going to need all the help we can get." said Josh.

"How about all of us get back together tomorrow?" said Josh.

"Sounds, like a plan" said Skylar. Taking shots of liquor back to back.

"It was honor to meet you Skylar." said Levi.

"You too." said Skylar.

She grabbed her leather coat, and gave Josh a hug and told him she would see him tomorrow.

She headed out of the door, and got in her car. As Skylar got in her car she was feeling a little intoxicated. As she drove, all she could think about was what had happened to her grandfather. As she was driving, she noticed a car behind her. The car flashed its lights on high beams. Then all of the sudden, the car sped up, really fast trying to run Skylar off the road. She tried to keep her car in the road. Right beside her was her gun. As they came up closer to Skylar, she opened her window and shot directly at them.

They shot back at Skylar, it was two guys dress in black suits, and they were in Bowler's mob.

They were right behind her. Skylar figured out a plan to get rid of them. There was a cliff nearby. Skylar's plan was to run them off the cliff. As they got closer to Skylar, she shot multiples times at the mob. They didn't see what was coming, Skylar quickly turned and they ran off the cliff. The car exploded into flames. *Game over*, she thought.

While she was on the highway, she decided not to go back to the mansion. She would go back to Killermike's warehouse. She decided that she would do some gun training. All Skylar could think about, was how Mr. Bowler had sent his goons to kill her. His goons ended up dying trying to kill her.

Skylar took off her leather coat and grab a bottle of Jack Daniels that Killermike had left there.

Skylar sat there drinking and thinking about her grandfather. She grabbed her gun and started flipping while shooting and landing on her feet. She started doing a lot of her martial arts moves with the gun in a flash. She then took a seat, she was starting to get tired.

As she rested tears fell from her eyes. Skylar felt like she was not to supposed to cry, but they came anyway. As she looked, a beam of light started to form; it was like her grandfather was coming from heaven above. Skylar started to rub her eyes, to see if it was real. She thought that she was just drunk.

"Oh my god grandfather is it you?" said Skylar.

"Yes it is me." said her grandfather.

"How can this be?" said Skylar.

"God and the angels from heaven above sent me here to give you a message." he said. "Skylar you are not alone, god and the angels above are with you."

"Grandfather, I always kept faith, even with every battle I faced I never gave up." said Skylar. "But I regret not being able to save you."

"Skylar, it was my time to go." said grandfather. "God gave me a higher calling. He has also given you a power of great strength and you also have a purpose. Your purpose is to protect the ones you love and help the ones who need you. The cross that you wear on your neck is only given to the gifted ones. Skylar it has always been your destiny, to fight for what is right in the world. My dear child, why are their tears coming from your eyes?"

"Because I wish that you were still here with me always." said Skylar.

"Skylar, I'll always be here with you." said grandfather.

"Grandfather, you were telling me that the cross Ms. Rosa gave me has special powers." said Skylar.

"Yes, this necklace was made centuries ago by the angels of heaven, to give to one of the gifted, to defeat the evil in the world." said the grandfather. This special cross was also given to MS. Rosa's daughter who is in heaven, now."

"If she was gifted why is it that she's not here?" said Skylar.

"She too had a higher calling, she is a gateway to help lost souls get into heaven." said grandfather.

"Remember to never give up." said the grandfather. A bright light appeared like a glow from heaven.

"Grandfather, I love you." said Skylar.

He threw his hand up and waved goodbye, Skylar waved goodbye back to him. Skylar knew if she told anyone that they wouldn't believe her. She decided that she would head back home to the mansion in the morning. She didn't want her father to smell the stench of alcohol on her. She got a blanket and cosied up on the couch where she fell asleep.

The next day Skylar got up and got ready to return back to the mansion. Before, Skylar got ready to leave she grabbed her leather coat that was Killermike's. As she grabbed the door, she glanced back, she still couldn't believe her grandfather came down as an angel. She knew that she couldn't tell anyone they wouldn't believe her. She closed the door, and headed to the car.

When she arrived at the mansion, Monty and Ms. Rosa heard her car coming in.

"Dad have you been worry about me?" said Skylar. "I decided to stay at Killermike's last night."

"Why?" Said Monty.

"After I left Josh and Levi, two guys that from the mob tried to run me off the highway." said Skylar.

Monty grabbed his daughter and hugged her. "Skylar I wouldn't know what I'll do if I ever lost you." he said

"Dad, This is what I was trained to do." said Skylar.

"I will not rest until Mr. Bowler pays for what he has done." said Skylar.

"Skylar, I know you have been trained by the best but you're up against something that will take more than just you." said Monty.

"Dad, Josh, Levi and I are going to find Mr. Bowler no matter what it takes." said Skylar. Skylar's phone began to receive a text, it was from Josh.

Meet us outside! Going to Mr. Bowler's old neighborhood.

Skylar laced up her leather boots, loaded her 9mm. Ready to leave out the door. Monty told his daughter to be safe.

"I will." said Skylar.

Skylar got into the van. They sped off to the old neighborhood.

"What do you think we will find? Skylar asked.

"Hopefully, clues of where Mr. Bowler is, his plan for Clark Enterprises." said Levi.

"Does everyone have their weapons? We don't know what's waiting for us." said Josh.

They both said yes.

When they arrived at Mr. Bowler old neighborhood they were amazed. It looked like a ghost town. The houses looked abandoned, as if no one lived there for decades. As Josh turned the van into the neighborhood, they saw people looking out the windows, wondering why they were there.

Suddenly, Josh saw a store that also looked abandoned; it looked like someone just went inside. Josh stopped and parked the van at the side of the store. Everyone got out of van. As Josh grabbed the screen door it screeched loudly. As Josh looked up, a Smith and Wesson rife was pointed directly on him.

"I wouldn't do that if I were you." said Skylar as she pointed her gun at him.

"Drop your guns." said the man.

"Not a chance." said Skylar

"Do you know who she is?" Josh asked

"No, who is she?" said the man.

"She is the owner of Clark Enterprises and she also killed most of Bowler's mob." said Josh.

"So I suggest you put your gun, down or you will be wearing it, by the time I'm through with you." said Skylar.

"Yeah, I've heard of you." said the man. "Honestly, I don't want any trouble. I'm slowly, putting the gun down."

Levi grabbed a chair and pushed him down in it. "Do you know what we are here for?"

"For Mr. Bowler." said the man.

"Bingo." said Levi.

"He will kill me if I tell you where he is." said the man.

"What is your name?" said Skylar.

"My name is Mario Sanchetz. My family and I have been tortured by Mr. Bowler for years. We have been forced to do as Mr. Bowler, says in order to live in our homes."

"You never tried leaving?" said Josh.

"No" said Mario. "But, I have the feeling he knows that you're here. Mr. Bowler has eyes everywhere. It will not be long, before he sends someone after our whole neighborhood. Please help us."

"First, we need to know if there are any plans or secrets that Mr. Bowler is hiding." said Josh.

"Yes but first before I tell you, you have to get my family and the rest of the neighborhood out of here." said Mario.

As, Mario and Josh were talking, Skylar noticed something in the corner of the store. It looked like a person. So Skylar went over to see what or who it was. It was an old lady, with a black silk veil on. The woman said to her "finally you have come." Skylar sat down beside her.

"What do you mean?" said Skylar.

"The prophet said that a woman with gifted powers would save the world from chaos and self-destruction. The cross you carry is powerful." said the woman.

Mario spoke up "She is my mother, she always spoke about a women that is gifted with power from heaven who will save the world from destruction and evil."

"She's telling the truth." said Skylar. "I'm that person."

"I knew there was more to you. You can move as fast as lighting, killing several men at one time." said Josh. "I just knew there was something special about you."

"Me too." said Levi.

"Enough about me, we need to know what Bowler is hiding."

"Can you promise to get everyone safely away from here?" said Mario.

"Josh, do you think you can get your friend from the CIA to get these people away from here safely?" Skylar asked.

"I'm on it now." said Josh.

Josh was on his cell phone, taking to Amanda from the CIA explaining what was going on. She told Josh she was on her way.

"It's done. Your family and neighborhood should be safe. My friend Amanda is on her way."

"Mr. Bowler has a secret room." said Mario.

"Where?" said Josh.

Mario walked to the wall behind the counter in the store. He pushed a button and the wall opened up. Skylar, Josh and Levi entered the room. The room had a foul smell. The walls were covered in blood, newspaper clippings and pictures of Skylar from when she was a little girl right up to adulthood.

As, Skylar looked around she started to get a flashback to the day her grandfather died. Mr. Bowler was injured but because of his goon, Brian let him get away. He otherwise would have been killed. Skylar was so hurt that she didn't kill Mr. Bowler that she promised herself that she would get her revenge. As Josh and Levi looked around the room they noticed a bag with blood on it. Inside the bag they found money along with another bag that was filled with a white substance. Under a desk, they found papers with names of soldiers from the army. Soldiers that worked for Mr. Bowler.

"This is really big." said Levi. "We really are going to need a lot help and weapons."

"But first, we need to get these people out of here." said Levi.

Skylar kept staring like she was in a trance. Josh asked her if she was OK.

Skylar finally snapped out of it. "I'm fine. I think the smell of this room is getting to me. We need to get out here"

As they came out of the secret room all the people in the neighborhood were there, clapping and praising them. The CIA had arrived to put them in witness protection, so they would be safe.

"Josh." said Agent Amanda. "Nice to see you."

Agent Amanda told her guys to get all of the people out safely into the cars.

"So, you are the amazing Skylar Clark, and the owner of Clark Enterprises?" said Agent Amanda.

"Yes, I am." said Skylar.

"Nice to meet you." said Agent Amanda.

"This is Levi, he's a friend of ours, and he is helping us find Mr. Bowler, he used to work for Mr. Bowler and he killed his entire family." said Josh. "Our mission is to find him, anyway possible."

"Are you sure about that?" said Agent Amanda.

"Yes." they all said.

"We are on your side. Don't hesitate to call us." said Agent Amanda. "But from what I've heard about you, Skylar Clark, I know, you're capable of getting him."

"So what have you found so far?" said Agent Amanda.

Josh told her what they had found, and Agent Amanda sent some of her guys to investigate the secret room and retrieve the evidence that was found.

"Don't worry Skylar he will be found soon." said Agent Amanda.

"Soon is not good enough." said Skylar. "We are about go find him now."

"Well whatever you do, remember the CIA is on your side." said Agent Amanda.

"Josh, you have my number." said Agent Amanda.

Chapter Two

Everyone from the CIA left with the people from the old neighborhood. The people waved at them with smiles on their faces. For the first time in years, they were happy. Skylar waved back, with joy in her heart for them.

"Are you all ready to go?" Levi asked.

They all said yes.

"First, we have to get all our weapons together, and get a plane to find Mr. Bowler." said Josh.

"Before I leave I need to say goodbye to my family." said Skylar.

They dropped Skylar off at the Clark's Mansion. She told them to pick her up whenever they were ready.

As Skylar walked into the house past memories came flooding back. She saw her grandfather shot by Mr. Bowler. A tear came from her eye. She looked around to see if she could find her dad. She found Monty in her grandfather's office, which was now Monty's office. He was sitting at his desk.

"Dad!" said Skylar.

"Skylar! Where have you been?" said Monty.

"Josh, Levi and I decided to go after Mr. Bowler." said Skylar.

"Skylar do you think, you can win this battle?" said Monty.

"Yes, I know I can." said Skylar.

"This is a suicide mission." said Monty.

"Before I came here we went to Mr. Bowler's old neighborhood to try and find him. We saved the people that were living there. Mr. Bowler had threatened their lives for years." said Skylar.

"Where are they now?" said Monty.

"They are with the CIA." said Skylar. "We also found a secret room in the convenience store. Mr. Bowler planned to take over Clark's Enterprises. There was blood everywhere and we found bags with money and some sort of white powder. Josh contacted the CIA to tell them about what we found. They ensured us that that they would be there for us."

"Skylar, I know something about Mr. Bowler." said Monty. "The last time that you talked to Rico, he discussed something about the army."

"Large amounts of weapons have gone missing from the army" said Monty. "There a traitor in the army who works for Mr. Bowler. This is a battle, you need as many people's help as possible"

"Your right Dad and I plan on taking it." said Skylar. "Dad, I need you to be in charge of the company."

"Skylar, will you promise me, you will come back safely?" said Monty.

"Dad, I promise." said Skylar.

"I lost your mother, I won't lose you too." said Monty.

Skylar gave her father a hug and went to Killermike to train at the warehouse before leaving to go overseas. Josh and Levi found a pilot next. Levi knew that he sold guns of all kinds illegally. Dan Fisher was the guy to see, in his house were guns of all kinds. Dan kept his guns in his basement. They followed Dan to the basement.

"Whatever ya'll guys need I have it." said Dan

Josh told Dan they needed everything and handed Dan ten thousand dollars. Josh and Levi loaded up everything in the van. Skylar was at Killermike's training and after she was through, there was a box that she decided to carry the suit with her, also in the box were some dusty parachutes. Skylar carefully dusted them off; also she had guns that were Killermike's. As, Josh and Levi got to Killermike's, Josh told Skylar that they had a pilot waiting. Skylar got everything together.

Josh said He'll stop a local store to get food for the long flight. Then Josh, Levi and Skylar got ready to board the flight.

***

At the army, Kenny and Scott were interviewing some of the soldiers. Marcus disappeared from the soldiers. He called Mr. Bowler.

"Why are you calling me at this time?" said Mr. Bowler.

"It seems like Kenny Clark is a reporter, looking for information about the missing weapons, he has a friend with him named Scott, who is a photographer." said Marcus.

"Have a couple of soldiers that work for me show the photographer something." said Mr. Bowler. "While entertaining Kenny!"

So the soldiers did what Mr. Bowler wanted, they told Scott they had something to show him. They brought him into a room and a soldier grabbed him around the neck, the camera went down, and the solider suffocated him with a white cloth drenched with chloroform. They dragged him out of the army and on a truck to Mr. Bowler.

After, talking to the soldiers, Kenny realized Scott was gone. He started looking around.

He started looking around, asking soldiers if they have seen him. Everyone shook their heads no. So, he went to talk to the sergeant about what was going on.

He told the soldiers that people just don't disappear all of a sudden. The sergeant said he would try to get to the bottom of it.

Kenny decided to call New World. He told them what had happened to Scott, they told him to keep searching for clues.

Skylar, Josh and Levi were in the air. A few hours later the pilot started having trouble with plane.

"This can't be happening." said Josh.

Levi went to see why the plane was having problems all of a sudden. Levi overheard the pilot talk to someone on the phone.

It sounded like the pilot had a plot to kill them all on the plane including himself. As he got closer to hear, he heard the man talking to the pilot. He told him to kill everyone, if Skylar would not sign over Clark Enterprises to him.

Levi quickly rushed back to Skylar and Josh. Levi told them, he heard the pilot talking to Mr. Bowler and how he had planned on killing them all, if Skylar decided not to sign over Clark Enterprises over to him.

"I will never sign over my grandfather's company." said Skylar. "We are not going to die. Seems like those parachutes I brought will come in handy."

Skylar, Josh and Levi got what they could carry with them and prepared to jump. Looking out Josh told Skylar he wasn't sure if he could go through with it.

"Josh, yes you can, you have to believe." said Skylar.

As the plane kept moving Skylar spotted a village, Skylar told them to jump towards the village.

They joined hands and jumped. The pilot looked mad and upset they had gotten away.

Suddenly, the plane went down into the river. They all fell from the sky and landed safely. They all hugged each other and began the long walk to the village.

***

Clark Enterprises, the company that owned the plane, contacted Monty telling him that the plane Skylar was on was missing.

"What do you mean the plane is missing?" Monty demanded. "Planes just don't disappear; you find my daughter and her friends."

The guy from the company told him that they were trying everything. Monty told him that was not good enough and hung up. He called the CIA and they agreed to help him find her.

***

Skylar, Josh and Levi were still walking and were getting tired; soon they were close to a village. As they made it, they noticed it was so beautiful; the kids were playing among the beautiful flowers and trees.

A lady stopped and asked them if they needed help.

"Yes." said Skylar. "The plane that we were on just crashed in the river, not too far from here, we need a place to stay until we can figure things out."

The woman agreed to the let the three of them stay with her.

Skylar noticed an army base close to the village. As the lady, looked up she said to Skylar, "It's sad what happened to that man that came to the army to take pictures about the missing weapons."

"Do you know what that man's name was?" said Skylar.

"I think his name was Scott and he was with a man name Kenny Clark." said the woman.

"Was he from New World Times?" said Skylar.

"Yes." Said the woman. "That man has searched and searched for his friend but he couldn't find him. I think the army knows about everything."

Skylar began to think of how to get into the army without being recognized.

The woman told Skylar her name was Maria Cartel.

"Before you came here, I saw you coming." Said Maria.

"What do you mean?" Said Skylar.

"I have a gift, I can see these things." said Maria. "Let me know if you need anything."

"I will." said Skylar.

Skylar kept looking up far to the army base. Skylar looked into her bag, and found the army suit she had got from Killermike's warehouse. She knew it was time to find out what was going on.

"This is dangerous." said Levi.

"I'll be fine." said Skylar.

At the army base there was a meeting about finding Scott the photographer for the New World Times. As the meeting was ending Skylar seen Kenny go out the door, with no one behind him. She started to follow back, Skylar grabbed him before anyone could see.

"What seems to be the problem?" said Kenny.

"I'm your niece." said Skylar.

"My niece?" said Kenny.

Skylar quickly removed her hat and Kenny watched as her curls fell to her shoulders.

"Oh, my lord Skylar, you shouldn't be here." said Kenny.

Skylar, told Kenny about the plane and how the pilot had tried to kill them all. She told him that people in the army base were not to be trusted.

"Not again." said Kenny.

"What are you talking about?" said Skylar.

"I came over here for a story, instead I get caught up with Mr. Bowler again." said Kenny.

"Kenny, you couldn't possibly have known." said Skylar. "Is Rico here?"

"Yes." said Kenny.

"I'm going to try to get his attention." said Skylar.

Skylar put her hat back on, and got back into disguise.

"Skylar please be safe." said Kenny.

"I will." said Skylar.

At the CIA, agent Amanda Logan was informed that Skylar and her friend were on a plane that crashed.

"Were not buying that story." said Amanda. "We need to get everyone from the CIA together. We need to find these missing people."

She was showing them a picture of Skylar, Levi and Josh when she heard her phone ringing.

"Have you found their bodies yet?" said Mr. Bowler.

"You are not supposed to call here." she whispered.

"My dear, sweet Amanda." said Mr. Bowler. "I will call whenever I feel like it. So answer my question, have they found their bodies yet?"

"No." she said slowly.

"Are they going to see if they are still alive?" said Mr. Bowler.

"Yes." said Amanda.

"Good girl." said Mr. Bowler

"By you calling here, they could find out I'm working with you and blow the whole thing." said Amanda.

"Don't be so sure about that said" Mr. Bowler. "As long, as you follow what I say we should be fine. All we need to do is find the bodies and see if they are dead or alive. If not, resort to plan B. Get back to me when you have more information."

"Yes sir." said Amanda.

"That's sounds more like it." said Mr. Bowler.

The phone hung up and Amanda went back to work on the case.

At the army, Skylar's was still in disguise as a soldier name N. walker. She saw Rico going to the men's restroom; she started to follow him. Skylar entered and locked the door behind her. He felt something wasn't right.

"Why did you just lock the door?" said Rico.

She removed her disguise. "Rico it's me, Skylar."

"What the hell!" said Rico. "Skylar, why are you here, does your dad know you're here?"

Skylar sat down and told him the whole story.

"Skylar I wouldn't know what I would do without you." said Rico.

Rico finally told her to get back into disguise. Rico knew they would kill her if they found her.

"Have you seen Kenny yet?" said Rico.

"Yes." said Skylar.

"I need you to keep your eye on the sergeant." said Skylar. "I'm going to go to the sergeant's office to see what I can find out."

Skylar headed into the sergeant's office undetected. She looked around his office and saw a picture of the sergeant and a guy name Marcus standing beside Mr. Bowler. There were files near it, it was a file about soldiers who were under mind control and were successful at it. Also, there were plans to use those soldiers to take out Clark Enterprises. She heard footsteps so she hid in the closet.

The Sergeant placed some of the paperwork down and went back out of the door, she peeped out to see if he was gone. He was. Skylar quickly got away from the office. As she rounded the corner Rico grabbed her and pulled her to a quiet place where they were both hidden.

"They are plotting something he whispered, stay down."

They overheard the sergeant talk to the soldiers about what Mr. Bowler wanted them to do. To get as many soldiers as they could to see if they could withstand the mind control machine. There was a tin container that consisted of a liquid that was an antidote to reverse the mind control; it was given to the soldiers to put in the place in the sergeant's office.

"What is going on? Mind control? Is this what I'm hearing?" said Rico.

"Yes." said Skylar. "This is going to be a tough battle and we are going to need to contact the CIA on this one to help us."

"How do you know there is someone behind it?" said Rico.

"From what I know, the sergeant has only some soldiers under the mind control and he's in the early stages of it." said Skylar.

"Skylar, I can't understand, how you are not afraid of all of this." said Rico.

"I've been fighting since I was a little girl. I have seen it all said." Skylar. "I've lost loved ones and don't want to lose anyone again. It's my destiny to protect the ones I love."

"Your destiny, why do you say that?" said Rico.

"My grandfather came to me in spirit." said Skylar. "He told me that the angels from heaven are with me. The cross that was given to me from Ms. Rosa was a powerful cross only given to the gifted. So, I was chosen."

A tear came from Skylar eyes and Rico caressed her face and kissed her.

"I thank all the angels and heaven above for giving me a strong woman with a beautiful soul." said Rico.

"I love you." said Skylar.

"I have to tried to tell the others what I found out." said Skylar.

"But we are going to find out how to create a distraction to throw off the other soldiers who are under the mind control." Rico explained.

"You think you can get Kenny's attention to help?" said Skylar.

"I think I can." said Rico.

"Good." said Skylar.

Rico did a cartwheel in the army base, crawling low so that the soldiers wouldn't see him. He threw his hands up so, Kenny would see him.

"Excuse me everybody."

"What are you doing?" said Kenny.

"We need to create a distraction to get Skylar out of here." said Rico.

"What about pulling the fire alarm?" said Kenny.

"Then she can walk out unrecognized by the soldiers and disappear into the woods." said Kenny.

That's exactly what happened. Kenny put on protected gloves, so they couldn't trace any fingerprints and quickly pulled the fire alarm. He put the gloves in his pocket and had a lighter with a piece of paper and threw it into the storage room.

"I smell smoke." said Kenny.

The sergeant told everyone to leave the base.

Skylar got away quickly while they were distracted.

The sergeant and the soldiers who were under the mind control put out the fire.

***

At Clark Enterprises, Monty was at his desk calling as many people as he could to find his daughter. He was not going to rest until he found Skylar. Monty looked at his picture of Skylar, He said to himself, *I believe your still out there, I'm not going to lose hope*. The phone rang. It was agent Amanda.

"I'm calling you, to let you know my men are going to find out, what exactly went wrong with the plane and what happened to Skylar and her friends. Rest assured this will be investigated further."

"Take care." said Agent Amanda.

"You too." said Monty.

***

The sergeant at the army was conducting an investigation to see who set the fire. The sergeant said whoever set the fire will be caught and he told the soldiers to keep their eyes open.

Skylar made it back to the village and told Josh and Levi what had happened and how they must get out of the land of Impera.

"We must contact special forces." said Levi.

Levi went to Maria the woman who allowed them to stay in village.

Maria was sitting down in the garden, and before Levi could speak. Maria said "I know what you are looking for. You want to find a way to contact Special Forces to help get you out."

"Yes! How do you know?" said Levi.

"I know everything." said Maria. "There is a building with a phone line to contact America."

"Thanks." said Levi.

Levi ran to contact the government; he contacted a friend of his in the government to make sure that no one knows who were associated with Mr. Bowler. What Levi didn't know was that the CIA was already looking for them. Skylar was in her small room, thinking about Rico and what might happen to him. She was worried that he might turn out like the other soldiers.

Levi got his friend in the government to see about sending help down to Impera. He told Levi he would send someone and that he would tell the government about it.

59

Skylar had a decision to make - to leave Impera or stay and fight.

They had to get Kenny and Rico out of the army; it wouldn't be long before they found out about Kenny. She paused for a moment thinking to herself, *I should go back to the army base to rescue my uncle and boyfriend.*

At the army, the sergeant and Marcus questioned Kenny about his whereabouts. He explained he was in the bathroom with a stomach problem. He said he smelled fire and shouted fire.

The sergeant said to Marcus "What do you think?"

"I think he's lying." said Marcus.

"So who else is working with you." said Marcus.

"No one." said Kenny. "Honestly."

"Let's see about that." said Marcus.

Marcus got on the cell phone. "Mr. Bowler, I have Kenny Clark here."

"Hell no man." said Kenny. "You are supposed to be the US Army."

"We have our own plans and agenda." said the sergeant.

"Our goal is to do as Mr. Bowler directed." said the sergeant.

"So what are you going to do with me?" said Kenny.

They laughed and said that it was up to Mr. Bowler to decide.

"That is not fair" said Kenny.

"This is not fair, you shouldn't have come here." said the sergeant.

"That's exactly right." said Mr. Bowler.

"I haven't figured out what I'm going to do with you Kenny." said Mr. Bowler talking loud on speakerphone.

"To tell you the truth, you should have died in the battle at Clark Enterprises." said Mr. Bowler.

"I can use you again, maybe to get Skylar." said Mr. Bowler.

"You leave my niece out of this." said Kenny.

"There is no chance in hell, I will do that." said Mr. Bowler. "The company that I want is Clark Enterprises. I have Skylar Clark right where I want her."

"Bowler, if you touch my niece I swear I will…" said Kenny

"Swear, you will do what?" said Mr. Bowler.

"What did you do for your boy Scott?" said Mr. Bowler.

"Where is he?" said Kenny.

"I had some of my men kill him." said Mr. Bowler.

Kenny cried with tears of rage. "He didn't do anything."

"No, he was in the wrong place at the wrong time." said Mr. Bowler.

Chapter Three

Skylar was ready to leave to go back to the army base.

"This is too risky." said Levi

"I'll take my chances." said Skylar

Maria went to Skylar and told her to have something to eat before she left.

Josh told Skylar she would need to keep her strength up.

She agreed she would stay. You could hear the music beating from the drums, laughter and singing. There was plenty of food and people from the village.

Maria gave Skylar, Josh and Levi something to eat, the kids were chasing each other and laughing. A little girl came over and took Skylar's hat off her head gave it to Skylar. Putting a flower in her hair, Skylar started to smile and thanked her with a hug.

Skylar told Levi and Josh she would leave as it turned night. When night came Skylar was still in disguise as a soldier. She snuck around the army base, seeing if any soldiers were around. She told Levi and Josh the coast was clear. Skylar, Josh and Levi went in with their guns by their side. As they thought they heard someone coming, they backed against the wall. Skylar carefully stuck her head out and said the coast was clear. They took a left turn and looked around with their guns in the air.

The saw an open door and noticed that Kenny was tied up on a chair. She knew they were ready to kill him. Skylar cut the rope with a pocket knife. Kenny told Skylar to save herself instead of worrying about him.

"Kenny, listen to me, we are family and family stick together no matter what." said Skylar.

"Skylar, I don't know if I can take it anymore." said Kenny.

"Take what?" said Skylar.

"Everywhere I go I'm bring trouble." said Kenny.

"Kenny, you have to realize that we will always be targeted, because of who we are, the Clark Family. You have to fight to live in this world to make it." said Skylar.

She finished cutting the ropes and rescued him. Skylar handed Kenny a gun from her hip. She had one in her hands carefully creeping in the hall. Levi and Josh found out where the rest of the soldiers were. They were in a meeting in a large room, some were looking as they were possessed by something. There was a machine with one soldier lying under it. There was a guy in a white coat working the machine. They were checking to see if the machine was working.

"We need to get out of here." said Kenny

"I'm not leaving without Rico." said Skylar.

"Are you crazy?" said Kenny. "This army base is surrounded by soldiers under the influence of mind control. How are we going to get Rico without being seen?"

Before he knew it, she was gone out of site.

"What are we going to do?" said Kenny.

Josh said to watch out to see if anyone was coming.

Levi said "Don't worry Kenny we got you."

Skylar got in line with the other soldiers and tapped Rico on the shoulder and whispered to him. "You need to come with me."

"How are we going to do that? Said Rico

"Follow my lead." said Skylar.

There were two soldiers guarding the back of the entrance. Skylar told Rico, to tell them that they had to go, that his friend had fallen ill.

"Let's check him out." said the soldiers.

At that time, Skylar worked at the speed of lighting, kicking the soldier several time in the stomach and head. She grabbed the other soldier by the neck and killed him on contact. Rico looked like he was in shock.

"Rico." said Skylar. "Rico, snap out of it. We've got to go, before the others find out and come to their senses."

Skylar grabbed Rico and told the others to come with her. They got to the door of the army base.

Mr. Bowler was there with Marcus. Skylar had her gun and was prepared to shoot. Marcus got in front of Mr. Bowler and shot at Skylar. Skylar flipped fast out of the way and escaped.

The soldiers were possessed under the mind control, but suddenly a helicopter arrived. It was agent Amanda Logan from the CIA and she had two CIA agents with her. As she stepped out of the helicopter, her hair was flowing in the wind.

"Mr. Bowler, I see that you're out of breath." said Agent Amanda. "She's been here?"

"Yes." said Mr. Bowler.

"I think you're losing your touch." said Agent Amanda.

"Not at all, I have a secret weapon." said Mr. Bowler. "It's with them. Rico is controlled by me."

"Rico?" said Agent Amanda. "You put her boyfriend under the mind control? Well Mr. Bowler maybe I was wrong about you."

"Wrong, indeed." said Mr. Bowler.

"The plan that I have set, is that Rico is under my mind control, when he reaches America, then time will come for me to conquer Clark Enterprise." said Mr. Bowler. "Rico will do as I order, there is nothing Skylar Clark can do to stop my mind control."

Mr. Bowler started to laugh and grabbed Agent Amanda by the arm, would you like to have a drink with me?"

"I would love to." said Agent Amanda as she pulled out her gun and shot both of the men around her.

***

Skylar, and the rest of them were out of sight. They heard a plane located on the other side of the bridge. The bridge was kind of rocky and old.

"Skylar are you sure, we should do this?" said Josh.

"I'm sure." said Skylar as she kissed the cross in her hands.

Levi was holding up Rico up as he wasn't feeling well. He wondered what they should do with him.

"You will have to leave him near the tree here. We will come back to get him." said Skylar as she wiped the sweat from Rico's forehead. "Let's go."

They all went across the bridge slowly as possible. The bridge was rocking and piece of wood, fell as they looked down, they could see the river flowing fast. Skylar told them to stay calm.

The door on the plane opened and a man said "Are you Skylar Clark?"

"Yes!"

"I was sent by the government to take you back to America." said the man.

She noticed the pilot inside the plane and saluted him.

"Don't call me, sir." said the man. "My name is Agent Will Douglass."

"Okay Will but I can't leave just yet." said Skylar.

"Why not?" said Agent Douglass.

"My boyfriend Rico is over that bridge, sick, and I need to rescue him before I leave." said Skylar.

"How are you going to do that, he can barely stand." said Levi

"I'm going to try to get him over here." said Skylar.

"Skylar, we have help to take us back to America." said Kenny. "How do you know, they haven't put mind control on him and he's fighting for it not to control him?"

"I don't know." said Skylar. "If it is I will help him all I can."

"Skylar, I love you, you are my niece, but have you lost your mind?" said Kenny.

"I haven't lost my mind, I have love in my heart and I won't let anyone take that love away from me." said Skylar as she moved slowly across the bridge.

"We have to do something." Josh said

Levi asked Agent Douglass If he had something to throw down from the plane to carry Skylar and Rico up. The pilot told them that he did.

Agent Douglass told Levi and Josh to get in. Skylar had almost slipped off the bridge, she held her composure and eventually made it.

"I came back for you Rico." said Skylar.

"Skylar." Rico whispered slowly.

"I need you to get up, we need to make it across this bridge." said Skylar.

Rico carefully got up and Skylar held on to him, as they slowly crossed the bridge, it started to rock, Skylar tried to hold on to him, But she felt as she was losing her grip. Suddenly in the air a rope came down. Skylar grabbed the rope with her right arm and hooked it tightly to her belt buckle as the bridge fell piece by piece. Skylar shouted at them to pull her up.

They were now on their way to America.

Agent Douglass got on his plane and contacted the government to let them know they had gotten them up safely.

"Good job Agent Douglass, see you soon" said the president.

"Thank you" said Agent Douglass.

Monty was informed that his daughter and her friends were rescued and were coming back to America. Monty was happy. He told Ms. Rosa and Bertha Ann the good news.

"The angels are still with her." said Ms. Rosa.

"Why do you say that?" said Monty.

"Skylar, has a gift." said Ms. Rosa.

"She's been trained very well by Kiana and Killermike." said Monty.

"Believe it or not Skylar was chosen to do some amazing things to protect the people she loves." said Ms. Rosa.

"Is there something you're not telling me?" said Monty.

Bertha Ann spoke to Ms. Rosa "I think you better tell him."

"Do you remember the necklace with the cross?" said Ms. Rosa.

"Yes I do." said Monty.

"That necklace has great powers." said Ms. Rosa. "Only the gifted can wear it. The angels from above chose Skylar."

"You know I kind of felt that Skylar's fighting style was powerful, it's nothing like I have ever seen before." said Monty. "How did you know this?"

"My daughter was also gifted" said Mrs. Rosa. "And so am I. The angels called her to do something much greater, she agreed to take spirits up to heaven. She is now an angel. She visit me from time to time."

"So you see spirits?" said Monty. "Do you ever see dad?"

"He does stops by sometimes" said Ms. Rosa. "He is proud of you all."

"Does dad mention anything about my wife Rachael?" said Monty.

"Yes! He's says, she has been watching you and protecting you and Skylar" said Ms. Rosa. "She has been watching Skylar grow from a child to a young woman."

Monty was trying not to cry, but he grabbed his handkerchief and held it right close to him.

"That's all I wanted to hear." said Monty. "Thank you Ms. Rosa."

"Ms. Rosa and Bertha Ann, I think we should have a welcome home party." said Monty.

"Let's get started." said Bertha Ann.

***

Skylar and everyone were on their way to Clark mansion, Skylar told Rico he needed to go to the hospital

"No." Rico said quietly.

"We're getting him to hospital." said Agent Douglass.

They took him to Lance Medical Hospital where Skylar was born.

As the plane landed they hurried out taking Rico and putting him on a stretcher. The nurses quickly carried him off. One nurse stood with Skylar asking questions, Skylar gave her all the information she needed. Agent Douglass, Josh, Levi and Kenny all sat in the waiting room. Skylar sat by Rico's side.

The doctor came in and asked for her to wait. The doctor conducted tests on Rico, to figure out what was going on with him. They stayed for hours. Skylar went to sleep in the waiting room. The doctor stopped and took a second look. He felt that he knew the young lady. Then a flashback hit him. He remembered helping to deliver a baby girl whose mother died after giving birth to her. The baby girl's father was Monty Clark and Tony Clark was the grandfather Tony Clark helped raise the little girl. He looked at her and saw that she looked just like them.

"Miss?" said Dr Rice.

"Oh, hi doctor I had to go to sleep." said Skylar.

"That's quite alright." said Dr Rice. "I remember you."

"You remember me?" said Skylar.

"You're Skylar Clark?" said Dr Rice "I remember when you were first born. I was the doctor that helped with your delivery."

"It's nice to meet you." said Skylar.

"I know that you are very concerned about Rico. We are still testing him." said Dr Rice. "My advice to you and your friends is that you go home and get some rest."

"I think your right Dr Rice" said Skylar.

So everyone decided to go to the Clark's Mansion. On the way to the Clark's mansion Kenny thought to himself that he hadn't seen his brother since their father died. He was nervous about returning home, after all the things he put his family through.

 As they came to the Clark's mansion, Skylar opened the door.

"Surprise! Welcome back." they all shouted

They were shocked; they were not expecting a welcome back party. As everyone was standing, Levi took one step back, Monty looked amazed.

"Monty!" said Kenny "Is that you?"

"The one and only." said Kenny.

Monty went up to him, shook his hand and gave him a hug. "I'm glad to see you."

Monty noticed that no one was in the mood, for the Celebration. "Is there something that you want to tell me?"

"Dad, there is a lot I have to tell you." said Skylar.

So, Skylar told him everything, about the army having soldiers under mind control and Mr. Bowler being behind it all, and that Rico was put under the mind control, and was very ill in the hospital fighting it.

"Dad, I hope Rico will be ok." said Skylar.

"I hope so too." said Monty.

Levi said "What we need to worry about is the big invasion that Mr. Bowler is about to unleash on Clark Enterprises."

"We have help on our side" said Josh. "We just have to be careful about what help we are going to get."

"We know we cannot contact the CIA." said Skylar. "They are working with Mr. Bowler."

"Hold up, CIA and Agent Amanda?" said Monty.

"Yes." said Skylar.

"She called me, when your plane went down and told me she would not stop searching until she found you." said Monty.

"She wasn't searching for us to ensure our safely. She was doing that for Mr. Bowler." said Skylar.

"When, we escaped from the army, we saw agent Amanda talking to Mr. Bowler." said Skylar. "We then recognized a plane. It was agent Douglass from the US government that was there to save us."

"You are lucky to be alive." said Monty.

"Yeah! We are." said Kenny. "Just thinking about it makes me just proud to be here. The one thing we should all do is cherish our lives."

"You're right Kenny." said Monty. "You never know what's coming next in life."

The others agreed.

Skylar took a picture of Rico from her pocket and willed him to get better.

All of a sudden Ms. Rosa spoke up really loudly. "I know ya'll had a long trip and you're starving. So let's eat."

After dinner, Skylar went to her room, took a shower and got ready to go to bed.

***

The next morning Lance Medical Hospital was very quiet. The doctor was doing his early morning patient checks. Checking their tests and well-being. He noticed something unusual coming out of Rico's room.

It was a man dressed in black holding a long needle. Dr Rice shouted for him to stop. He quickly contacted security. Security ran after him, he quickly pulled out his 9mm gun and started to shoot while escaping.

Dr Rice went to see Rico. Rico's heart rate began to drop; it also looked like he had been injected with something. Dr Rice and the nurses got his heart rate to stop dropping and had him stabilized. Dr Rice began to conduct more tests to find out what exactly was going on. The police were called about the man dressed in black who injected Rico. When the police came the doctor gave a brief description of what the man looked like.

***

At the Clark's mansion the phone rang. It was the doctor telling Skylar what had happened.

Skylar said "I'm on my way." She jumped in her car and sped away.

***

The doctor did several tests on Rico and couldn't find out what the man had injected him with. Skylar got to the hospital and rushed to see if Rico was alright. The doctor left them alone, and went to the other patients.

Later, Skylar heard one of the nurses telling someone that they couldn't come to Rico's room. She informed the nurse she was with the CIA. Skylar knew it was agent Amanda, Skylar searched around the room to find somewhere to hide. She hid in the bathroom in so that agent Amanda wouldn't see her. Agent Amanda entered Rico's room and sat down in the chair beside him.

"How are you Rico?"

Rico, lay there with his eyes closed. He didn't know she was there. She reached into her purse and tossed up a coin and let it fall to the floor. Rico started to blink his eyes, she tossed the coin up again, and he started to open his eyes.

"Who are you?" said Rico.

"I'm a friend of Mr. Bowlers." said Agent Amanda. "You know, Mr. Bowler?"

"No." said Rico.

"Do you remember the mission?" said Agent Amanda.

On hearing those words an echo came into his head, the mission.

Rico said "Yes! I remember the mission."

"Follow along with the Clark's family, when the time is right, you will do as Mr. Bowler ordered you." said Agent Amanda.

"Yes." said Rico.

"Or Mr. Bowler will order for you to be killed." said Agent Amanda.

"I will not fail the mission." said Rico.

"Good." said Agent Amanda.

At that time, the nurse came in the room and told Amanda she had to leave.

As she left the room, the nurse took Rico off to X-ray for more tests.

When they left the room, Skylar saw a surgeon's uniform in the closet, she quickly put it on and came out dressed in blue with a mask on. Agent Amanda was in the waiting room on the cell phone. Skylar walked right pass her without being noticed.

She got in the car as fast as possible to get to the Clark's mansion.

When she got back home, she told her father what was going on at the hospital.

"What mission?" said Monty.

"The mind control has taken over him." said Skylar.

"Skylar I told you, you should have left him." said Kenny. "Now he's going to kill us all."

"Kenny, this is her boyfriend we're talking about, he's a human being just like anyone else." said Monty.

"A human being, that is under mind control and a soldier too." said Kenny.

"That's doesn't matter." said Skylar. "I can get him help to get out of that. Our love can set him free."

She called Levi and Josh and told them about Agent Amanda. Josh told her he had found out that Agent Amanda had been kicked out of the CIA. They found out she had been working for Mr. Bowler. The CIA was looking for them. Agent Amanda and Mr. Bowler were obsessed with getting their hands on Clark Enterprises.

As they were on the road to meet Skylar they were suddenly bumped by an SUV. They started to speed up, but the SUV was steady on them. Then, there was a gun shot. Josh looked through his rear-view mirror it was agent Amanda, with some guys in black.

Josh said "Levi shoot them."

Levi got out, placed his gun through the window and began shooting. Levi aimed at the left tire of their SUV and shot. The SUV started to shift and it slowed them down. They quickly sped away.

Chapter Four

Josh and Levi were on their way to the Clark's mansion. Monty told Skylar they were going to have to keep a sharp eye on Rico, when he got out of the hospital. "We also have to figure out, how we are going to reverse the mind control effects."

"Dad, we're going to get to the bottom of it'" said Skylar.

"I hope so for your safely and everyone else's'" said Monty.

The phone rang. It was Dr Rice.

"I've been doing all the necessary tests. They were all negative and I see no traces of anything'" said Dr Rice. "I'm sending him home. It looks like he might have a small case of amnesia. So keep your eyes on him, see anything strange and give me a call."

"I will." said Skylar.

Skylar hung up the phone and was on her way to the hospital once again. As she was about to leave, Josh and Levi pulled up and informed Skylar what just happened to them.

"Skylar, we managed to run them off, we shot their tire, and sped back here." said Josh. "But we need to have a plan. We have to get Agent Amanda, before she gets us."

"It's going to be a hard task, but we will figure it out." said Josh.

"I have to go get Rico." said Skylar.

"Agent Amanda tried contacting Rico while he was in the hospital, she will try to contact him again." said Skylar. "If he is under mind control and Agent Amanda is working for him, we can get to her and capture her."

"That sounds like a plan" said Levi.

Skylar went back to Lance Medical Hospital. This time with a 27- Glock. She wasn't taking any chances with Agent Amanda. If she could she would capture her or kill her. She entered the hospital; the nurse had Rico ready to go.

She grabbed the wheelchair and took him to the car. As they got into the parking lot Skylar felt someone was following her, she looked back and didn't see anything. She didn't want to worry Rico, so she didn't say anything. She got Rico in the car and they headed back to the Clark Mansion.

When they got back to the mansion Ms. Rosa helped Skylar and Rico to Skylar's room to lay Rico down. Rico still needed rest and he was still under the mind control. Monty came to the room, and told Rico he was glad to see him.

"So how long is it you before the mind control in him will try to get to Clark Enterprises?" said Monty.

"If Agent Amanda is hoping for Rico to take it over for Mr. Bowler it shouldn't be long." said Skylar.

"We need to set up extra security codes for the security system." said Monty.

"Dad, I'll go out to Clark Enterprises, to make sure everything is set." said Skylar.

As Skylar was driving she felt like she was going to lose Rico because of the mind control. Mind control could make people do some crazy things. But she decided to think positively instead of negatively. Her focus was to protect Clark Enterprises.

At the Clark's mansion, Rico woke up and got out of his bed. He noticed that Skylar wasn't around. He grabbed Monty's car keys and jacket and headed out the door.

Monty and Kenny were in the mansion and didn't know he had left. As Rico was driving he started having flashbacks. It was from when he was in the army, he remembered being under the mind control machine and them doing something to him. He had one hand on the steering wheel and the other hand on his head. He slowed down. Then something triggered in his mind, there was no more pain. He started to drive to Clark Enterprises.

When he got to Clark Enterprises, he parked the car in an area where Skylar or no one else would know. Rico parked behind a security van. Some of the security got out of the van, one stayed in the van. Rico started to think how he could get inside Clark Enterprises without Skylar noticing he was there. He went to the security van.

"Excuse, me sir I'm looking for Fort Lane road. Could you tell me how to get there?" said Rico.

As he got out of the van, Rico knocked him out, put him in the van and took his uniform. He then put his body in the bushes, so no one could find him. He went into Clark Enterprises dressed as security.

At Clark Enterprises, security was providing extra protection to their security system. The Clark Enterprise security system was computerized and they had entered in a series of new codes in their system to alert them if a threat was detected or their system was being hacked. Skylar had her arms crossed and was listening to security giving their system a boost. She asked them if it could malfunction. They assured her she was 100% protected. In Skylar's head, she remembered what Gavin had did to help them. She also knew how to stop the hackers.

As one of the guys was putting in the codes in the security system, Rico was in a corner and saw what the codes were. He got out a pad from his jacket and wrote them down. He left unnoticed. He took off the uniform and drove back to the mansion.

At the Clark mansion, Kenny decided he wanted to see Rico. When he reached the door, he knocked twice but there was no answer. He opened the door and realized that Rico was no longer there. He rushed to Monty's office

"Monty, Rico is gone." said Kenny.

"He has to be here somewhere." said Monty.

Rico finally entered the Clark's mansion and returned the car back to the spot where it was. After searching for Rico, they decided to call Skylar. Skylar rushed on home. When she got home, she found Rico in the backyard. It looked like he was in peace, and did no harm to anyone. She went to show Monty and Kenny where he was. They looked amazed, they thought that the mind control had made him take off and turn evil.

Monty noticed tire tracks in the yard which was strange as none of the cars had been moved. He wondered if Rico had left at some point. Monty didn't want to hurt Skylar. It was better she found out for herself.

That night Rico was sweating profusely. The mind control had set in. Rico constantly tossed and turned in bed, his head was in so much pain. He felt that something was controlling him; someone was sending signals to his brain. It was Agent Amanda sending a signal to Rico with the mind control.

Rico got out of bed; he grabbed Monty's jacket and keys along with the notepad containing the Clark Enterprise security codes. He took them to give them to Agent Amanda.

Skylar heard a sound, it was Monty's car. A headlight flashed in the window. Skylar wondered why her father would be out at this time of night. As she looked, she noticed Rico was gone. She got up out of bed to look around. She saw that Kenny was sleep, so she went to her father's room. Monty was also there.

Skylar went back to her room to change her clothes and grabbed her gun. She remembered her father's car had GPS tracking on it. She decided to get into her car and track him down. She didn't want her dad or uncle to know that he had left.

She followed him, watching the GPS in her car. It gave her his destination. As Skylar was driving she started to recognize where he was going, she remembered Mr. Bowler's old business McCalla Inc. Rico went inside the building. Skylar parked the car, and snuck around the yard. She heard Agent Amanda.

Rico said "I have info on Clark Enterprises. I have the new security access codes for Clark Enterprises security system."

Rico was standing there in full attention like a soldier. Agent Amanda came over to him, grabbed him by the head and gave him a kiss. Skylar saw them kissing. She was furious. Her heart was thumping real hard, and then tears dropped from her eyes. Skylar knew that if she went in and killed Agent Amanda, she would not find out about Mr. Bowler whereabouts. She decided to go back to the mansion.

"Why did you kiss me?" Rico asked.

"Because it felt good." said Agent Amanda.

"You were not instructed to do that." said Rico.

"I do whatever I please." said Agent Amanda.

"I serve Mr. Bowler." said Rico.

"You say that, but you still have feelings for that Skylar." said Agent Amanda.

"Being involved with me could jeopardize the mission." said Rico.

"Just stick with the plan." said Agent Amanda.

"That is what I was instructed to do." said Rico.

"I will be watching and waiting." said Agent Amanda.

"I will report any valuable info to you, for Mr. Bowler." said Rico.

"Rico, I hope for your sake you don't have any love for Skylar Clark." said Agent Amanda. "Mr. Bowler, will kill her and the rest of the Clark family."

"I know." said Rico.

"So continue to play along." said Agent Amanda.

Skylar was at home in the mansion, crying. She took out a bottle of Jack Daniels out of her jacket. She cried her eyes out and then went to bed.

Rico drove back to the mansion, he put Monty's car back exactly where it was. He placed Monty's keys where they were on the kitchen counter. Skylar heard him come in. He went into the bathroom and changed into his clothes to go to bed in. He lay down by Skylar in the bed. Skylar looked up and then close her eyes too.

The next morning, Skylar got up. It was time for breakfast.

"I'm going to Killermike's to train. I should be back later. Take care Rico." said Skylar.

"I can take care of myself, I'm fine." said Rico.

"Well, since you're fine, you and Kenny should help me out at Clark Enterprises." said Monty.

"I can't wait to get my life back to normal." said Kenny.

"If you could call it normal." said Monty.

***

Skylar was at Killermike's working on her martial arts and shooting skills. She sat down, exhausted from her workout. She noticed a figure in the corner. It was her Grandfather. She ran to him.

"Grandfather, Rico is under mind control. Mr. Bowler did something to him overseas at the army. Last night, I saw him kiss a woman that works for Mr. Bowler. He even got into Clark Enterprises and stole the security codes to our access system." said Skylar.

"Skylar, Rico cares about you and loves you a great deal, he is under mind control which is leading him to think Mr. Bowler is good. You have to get him to break free and believe who he is again." said grandfather. "Skylar you have a lot of challenges to face, you are the future of Clark Enterprises."

"I know grandfather." said Skylar.

"You are strong. I know you can do this." he whispered as he slowly disappeared.

Skylar put her 9mm on her side and called Josh and Levi and told them about what she found out about Rico. Josh asked Skylar why she hadn't done something about this.

"Because I still love Rico, and I think we can come up with a plan to get him back to normal. There's got to be something at Mccalla. There has to be an antidote or something that can help cure Rico." said Skylar.

"Let's see if we can find anything that can lead us to Mr. Bowler or the antidote." said Josh. "Stay there, we'll come and get you."

Skylar sat outside waiting for Josh, listening to the birds and observing the beauty of the trees outside. It was quiet and peaceful, it was not as sunny, but you could feel a cool breeze coming through. Suddenly, Josh pulled up and Skylar hopped into the van.

As they were on their way to Mccalla Inc there was a man that looked like he was dead in the middle of the highway. The guy was black with a cowboy hat and a long beard. He was stiff. Levi got out of the van to see if he could identify the man. He had a wallet on him, his name was Richard Stamps. He was the guy who owned a farm near Mccalla.

Mr. Bowler always wanted his land. They pulled the man out of the road, put the cowboy hat on his face and said a prayer for him. Then got back in the van and got ready to go to Mccalla.

They parked the van, so that no one could see it. They walked and hid by the trees and bushes to hear what they were doing. Agent Amanda was talking to the men about the return of Mr. Bowler. She said she was going by a nearby airport to pick Mr. Bowler up, the two men were to accompany her, they got into the black car and left. Levi hurried across the yard to see if the coast was clear. It was.

"So, I guess we now know Mr. Bowler is coming home." said Skylar. "We need to find the antidote."

They went inside and found Mr. Bowler's desk. They found a deed with Richard Stamp's name signed on it.

Skylar turned to Levi and Josh. "Agent Amanda must have made him sign it before he died." She looked at the deed. "I'm so very sorry, I wasn't here."

"You couldn't have known." said Josh. "She will get what she deserves."

The found a stack of files. They were marked in red. Confidential. They kept looking and eventually found Rico's file It had what was injected into him along with a list of experimental drugs that were now in the United States. It was Amobarbital, a hypnotic sedative that induced amnesia.

When he was taken under the mind control machine, he was also injected with 2-CT2 which produced a dark, earthly visual pattern, that could make a person deadly with mind control. He could hurt anyone who stood in his way. There was one drug that could make him better. Propranolol - This calms the mind and allows it to function better.

Skylar said "Do you think that it will make Rico better?"

"I don't know Skylar." said Josh.

They looked around and found Propranolol, with an antidote called X- steno, which helped clear the mind. But if the body rejected it, it could be fatal. But using the Propranolol, before using the X-steno would help the body accept it.

Skylar gave the information to Levi. It looked like the CIA were heavily involved in this

"I can't believe this is true." said Josh.

"It doesn't surprise me one bit with all the chaos in the world today." said Levi.

"The world today is wicked and the world needs someone to make it better and to keep hope alive." said Skylar.

"We have to be ready to get out of here, before they come." said Josh.

"Get the van, and take a detour out of here." said Skylar.

They headed out another way. Mr. Bowler, Agent Amanda and the 2 guys came back. Amanda looked at the door. It was obvious someone had been inside. The two guys went to look around but couldn't see anything.

"So, what have you found out about Clark Enterprises?" said Mr. Bowler.

"We have found out they have updated their security system access codes." said Agent Amanda. "Rico, gave them to me after I signaled his brainwave with the transmitter."

"So, they don't know that Rico is doing things under our control?" said Mr. Bowler.

"I don't think so." said Agent Amanda.

"Amanda, I want you to signal Rico. Now let's see what happens." said Mr. Bowler.

***

"Is there something wrong?" Monty asked.

"I feel sick, do you have a bathroom?" said Rico.

"Yes, go down the hall to your right." said Monty.

Rico went in looking for a window. He got out and suddenly the pain stopped. He was on his way to Mccalla. He saw a man getting out of his car. He left his keys behind. Rico stole the car, and took off.

***

At Clark Enterprises, some of the employees were talking about the police being next door. That someone had stolen a poor man's car. When Monty heard he felt weird. Kenny was

88

organizing some files, putting them in place. Monty told Kenny to go check on Rico.

"Rico, you alright man?" Kenny asked as he opened the door slowly. The room was empty.

"The mind control is taking effect, he must have been called by someone." said Monty. "But who?"

"That's what I want to know." said Kenny.

The phone rang. Monty answered. It was Skylar.

"Skylar is Rico with you?" Said Monty.

"No, dad he's supposed to be with you." said Skylar. "What's going on? Are you still at the mansion?"

"We are at Clark Enterprises." said Monty. "I brought him here so he could help me out."

"Dad, Rico could harm someone with the mind control affecting him." said Skylar. "How did he get away?"

"He said his head was hurting and asked where the bathroom was." Monty explained. "That was the last we saw of him. He must have escaped through the window."

"I know who is signaling him" said Skylar. "It's Agent Amanda and Mr. Bowler. We went to Mccalla today, to see if we could find anything on Mr. Bowler. We found a body in the road, it was Richard Stamps. He owns a farm nearby."

"God bless him, I remember him. He wouldn't hurt a fly." said Monty.

"Agent Amanda forced him to give the land up; after which she must have killed him. He signed over the deeds but they killed him anyway."

"Someone needs to stop him." said Monty.

"Dad, I found an antidote for Rico, and some more things before leaving Mccalla." said Skylar. "But now Rico is gone. How will we find him?"

"If Mr. Bowler, has brainwashed Rico then things will get a lot worse." said Monty"

"He also has the new security access codes." Skylar told him. "Should we change them?"

"Leave them, as they are said Monty. Let him think he has the advantage. Rico is the key. We need him to regain control."

"Mccalla. Isn't that Mr. Bowler's old business?" said Kenny.

"Yes it is." said Monty.

"So, Agent Amanda is there." said Kenny.

"She's not the only one." said Monty.

"I can't believe Bowler is back." said Kenny.

"There is no telling what's in store for us." said Skylar. "And I was so close to curing Rico."

"Don't worry we'll get him back." Monty promised her.

"Why are we so worried about Rico?" said Kenny.

"For the same reason we were worried about you." Skylar snapped.

"I know. I'm sorry I didn't mean anything else." said Kenny.

"Kenny, grandfather really appreciated you. No matter how many times you messed up." said Skylar. "You were always trying to compete with dad."

"Skylar, that's enough." said Monty.

"No Dad, someone needs to tell him and it's time I spoke my mind."

"You two were father's perfect ones." said Kenny. "I admit I did mess up with the gambling, drinking and getting involved with the mob. It cost me my father. It still hurts so much to know that if it wasn't for me he would still be here."

"Kenny we know that you loved dad and he loved you." said Monty. "But now what's important is that we defend what he created. I'll be damned if Bowler thinks he can take it from under me. Clark Enterprises belongs to this family and we have to fight for it."

They all agreed to do whatever it took to take the company back.

Skylar went back to her office to sort some paperwork. A complaint had been lodged by an employee called Katie. She claimed another employee was acting strange and lashing out.

She went to his office to see if she could sort this out herself but when she opened the door she found the room was empty. She went to her father's office to see if he could locate the employee.

She explained the situation to him. He had not seen her so she told him that she was going to try and find the employee herself.

As Monty turned to leave he noticed sounds coming from Skylar's office. He opened her door and saw someone frantically working. It was clear that he was trying to hack the system but whatever he was trying was not working.

The man noticed Monty and lunged at him with a knife. Monty dodged the attack and punched the man in the head. He heard the knife drop. Just as the man was about to reach for the knife Skylar appeared again and shot him. He dropped to the ground, lifeless.

"Dad, are you alright?" said Skylar.

"I'm OK." said Monty His shirt was slashed from left to right. He sat down in the chair. Skylar sent Katie to get some ice from the lunchroom.

Skylar asked why the man was in the room and Monty explained that he was trying to hack the system.

She wanted to know who this man was. She reached into his pocket. She found a picture of him with his obviously pregnant wife along with a sonogram. Skylar reached into his other pocket and found a card with Mccalla and some sort of contract. It stated that Mr. Bowler would help pay for his taxes and mortgage if he was willing to become a test subject for his mind control machine.

She left the body and went to check the computer. From what she could tell he was trying to install some sort of spyware on the company's computers.

"Kenny, let me see the contract, that let Mr. Bowler perform tests of mind control on him." said Skylar. She called Josh and Levi and told them to come immediately.

Josh and Levi got to Clark Enterprises, they checked everything out and took some pictures to use as evidence later.

"It doesn't make any sense." said Levi. "Why send this guy when they already had Rico?"

"I don't know" said Skylar. "All I know is we are going to get to the bottom of this. I'm going home to change. Meet me at Killermike's."

***

Skylar reached the mansion and noticed Ms. Rosa was there waiting for her. It was a relief to see a kind, trustworthy face. She sat down with Rosa and told her everything that had happened. Rosa told her not worry, that everything would be alright in the end. She wished it was that simple. She made her way upstairs to change, her legs were heavy with worry.

Skylar put her belt around her waist and attached her guns- her 9mm and Glock- 27 along with enough bullets to bring down an army.

She went down stairs, jumped in her car and drove as fast as she could to Killermike's.

***

At Mccalla, Mr. Bowler was spending his spare time experimenting on Rico along with a woman who wore a white coat and lab glasses. Her name was Giovanna Delani, She was originally from Europe but had been lured into helping Mr. Bower with promises cash rewards. She hated Agent Amanda but she would put up with her if meant there was a wad of cash at the end of it.

Rico had been tied to a chair. His eyes were closed. It seemed like he was in a different world. On his head was a metal helmet with numerous wires attached to it. Giovanna sat with a clipboard monitoring his reactions.

"How's he doing?" Mr. Bowler asked.

"He's fine. His vitals are steady."

As Mr. Bowler was watching Giovanni his cell phone rang. It was one of his goons. He told him that the guy that was paying his taxes for was dead, he had messed up and now everyone at Clark Enterprises was on high alert.

"He was supposed to fulfill his side of the bargain. He failed. Now Bret White's family will pay the price." said Mr. Bowler.

Skylar, Josh and Levi had been near enough to hear the conversation. The goons went back inside to listen to Mr. Bowler's next orders.

"You know, what we have to do." said Skylar.

"We need to save the woman and her unborn child." said Levi.

"Let's go." said Josh. He had a computer in his van so he could locate the home address of anyone who worked for Clark Enterprises. They lived on Lakeside Drive in Lance County.

The house was beautiful, large and bright white. They saw his wife pacing back and forth. They could feel her sense of fear from outside. They approached the door and rang the bell.

"Hi, what can I do for you?" said Mrs. White.

"We have something important to tell you." They said as their heads fell.

"What is it?" she said.

"Your husband is dead Mrs. White." said Josh.

"You are crazy, get off of my property." she said and slammed the door.

"Skylar you need to tell her. You're the face of the company. She'll believe you." said Josh.

Skylar rang the doorbell again.

Mrs. White opened the door slowly. When she saw Skylar she knew something was wrong.

"Why are you here? What happened?"

"You're in danger Mrs. White you need to leave here now." Skylar explained.

"Not until you tell me what happened to my husband." Mrs. White demanded.

Skylar explained the whole story. When she was finished the prolonged silence made Skylar wonder if she believed her.

Tears began to run down her face. "I don't know what I'm going to do without Bret."

"I understand." said Skylar placing a hand on her shoulder. "I feel for you but if you want to meet your unborn son or daughter we need to get you out of here."

"I just need a few minutes to get ready." she explained.

She made her way through the house as fast as she could, grabbing anything that she might need. Skylar told her to leave the lights on. So it looked like she was still home. They ran to the van and sped off as quickly as they could.

***

Mr. Bowler's goons rounded the corner at Lakeside drive. Within 5 minutes the beautiful white house was engulfed in flames.

***

Skylar had an idea to keep Mrs. White safe. "There is a lady, I've heard of that has these safe houses for women who are pregnant and who fear for their lives. She helps them find a new identity."

"I don't know, if I can do this." said Mrs. White.

"You have to for your safety and for your unborn child." said Skylar.

"This is so hard." said Mrs. White.

The woman she heard of was Agatha Monroe. As they drove, they called her and she told them where to meet her.

There was a small alley between the stores. She asked them to meet her there as the cameras could pick up any mob members that showed up.

"Agatha Monroe?" said Josh. "This is Mrs. Leslie White."

The lady gave her a hug and said "I'm so sorry about your husband." She was crying and wiping tears from her eyes. "Mrs. White, you are going to make it. Be strong for you and your baby. I help a lot of girls that end up in situations like yours. Women who are on the streets with nowhere else to go."

Agatha had a hood on her head, she quickly took it off and her gorgeous curls fell from her head. Agatha was good person, a Christian that believed in helping to protect women and keep them safe. They left Mrs. White with the knowledge that she would be safe.

***

"We should go home and find out what Mr. Bowler is up to next." said Skylar.

The next day, Monty was watching the news. The newsreader said the house of the White's family on Lakeside Dr in Lance County had been set on fire. The police speculated that Mrs. Leslie White was in there and didn't make it out. A neighbor said that she was sitting in a chair by the window while the house went up in flames.

"Well looks like once again, Clark Enterprises has hit the news." said Monty.

"I wish they didn't air that." said Skylar.

Kenny was outside, sitting by himself in the garden. Skylar went to him.

"I wanted to check up on you to see if you are alright." said Skylar.

"I will be when Mr. Bowler is behind bars or killed." said Kenny.

"Kenny, I apologize, for the other day. I shouldn't have said all of the things I said."

"No, need for an apology. It was mostly me." said Kenny.

"Why don't we both accept each other's apology." said Skylar as she hugged him.

***

Mr. Bowler still had the army, under his control, even certain people in the CIA.

Mr. Bowler wanted to not only take over Clark Enterprises, but he also wanted to rule the world. His plan was to use the soldiers that were under mind control to be in his command to start war, with the government, the FBI, Navy and law enforcements who weren't under his mind control.

Now he had his special weapon, Rico was put in a special locked room in Mccalla. He was dressed in a white shirt and pants. Rico tried so many times to look for a way out, when he tried to open the door, it shocked him. They also had a camera inside, inside his room. They were tracking his every movement he made. It kind of felt like a prison, next to him was a guy, he spoke to him.

"They want to clear our mind and control us, like robots." said the guy.

"What are you talking about?" said Rico.

"They are using us. It's all about Mr. Bowler and his plan." said the guy.

"I don't think he's going to succeed with his plan." said Rico.

"You're wrong." said the guy. "Our brains are signaled to follow their commands. Sometimes my head really hurts. When, that happens it's not good. He will hook you under the machine again."

"So, you're saying it can lose its affects?" said Rico.

"Yes, for some who are lucky." said the man. "If the mind control fades away and you are still captured by him it's better to follow every command like you're in a trance."

The guy's name was Byson. He was a soldier; Mr. Bowler captured him as he was a strong guy and had amazing gun shooting abilities.

"You know, Bowler wasn't always like this." said Byson. "The anger and rage that's inside of him has something to do with what happen to him years ago."

"The only one I heard that knew about him was Tony Clark." said Byson.

"You, mean Skylar's grandfather knew about what happened?" said Rico.

"I heard he was tormented in his child hood and as he got older, he fed off on that to get revenge." said Byson. "It won' be long, before Skylar bust us out of here."

Rico was happy knowing that Skylar would rescue him. But he felt like he was a burden to her and maybe he could come up with a plan to get out. He also knew since they had tampered with his brain, he was in their complete control. He really didn't want to risk it.

***

Mr. Bowler was on his way back overseas to grab some illegal weapons. As his goons were driving they spotted Kenny. Kenny was driving from the video store; he wanted to get a movie that he liked to enjoy. As Kenny was driving he didn't notice the car that pulled up beside him.

Kenny sped with his mustang really fast, they were catching up with him and shooting. Kenny got his 9mm, gun and shot through the window of his mustang.

Kenny shot the guy on the passenger side, he died. The guy driving was still shooting at Kenny. Kenny was shooting back, all of a sudden; Kenny was hit in the shoulder. He hit the gas pedal and quickly lost them at the next exit.

Instead of going to a local hospital, he drove back to the mansion. As Kenny was driving he was in so much pain. The pain was really bad; the blood was rushing out of the wound. When he got to the mansion, he took the keys out of the car, and got out. He shut the door; blood was still dripping from his shoulder.

"Oh, my god what happened?" said Monty.

"Mr. Bowler's goons shot me." said Kenny.

Skylar ran to help Kenny and carefully sat him down.

"What is going on?" said Ms. Rosa.

"Ms. Rosa, can you go upstairs and get the first aid kit and a pair of tweezers out the bathroom?" said Skylar.

"Yes." said Ms. Rosa.

"I'm going to the kitchen to get the bottle of scotch." said Skylar.

Skylar grabbed 2 small glasses and the bottle.

Monty asked "Why are you getting two glasses?"

"One for me and one for him." said Skylar.

"Never mind, I asked." said Monty

"Kenny, do you want to go to the hospital?" said Monty.

"No." said Kenny.

Skylar, poured the scotch into a glass and gave it to Kenny. He drank it really fast.

"Skylar give me another." said Kenny.

Skylar poured another small glass and Ms. Rosa came downstairs with the first aid kit.

Ms. Rosa handed Skylar the first aid kit and tweezers. Skylar got ready to pull out the bullet. She had sterilized the tweezers. By the time she was ready to pull the bullet out Kenny had passed out. The bullet wasn't deep as she thought it would be so she was able to pull it out and bandage his arm.

Skylar headed for the coat rack and took Killermike's leather coat off the rack and put in on.

"Dad, I'm going to Killermike's, I'll be back soon." said Skylar.

"Skylar, be careful." said Monty.

As she was driving, she thought about Rico. Skylar loved Rico deeply and he loved her too deep down. Skylar thought to herself 'when is my life going to be normal.' After Skylar's grandfather died she felt a part of her was missing. She still felt like his death was her fault and she wanted revenge.

Skylar went inside Killermike's to get some figures to shoot outside, she placed some of the figures far away to test her aim.

Skylar got her gun and jumped and shot. It hit the figure right in the head. She did several more, until she was tired. She decided to go back inside Killermike's. She grabbed a beer from the fridge and sat down.

She called Josh and told them to meet her at Mccalla's at midnight. Skylar wanted to know what they were doing to Rico, and what they had planned for him, besides taking over Clark Enterprises.

So at midnight, Skylar and Levi were at Mccalla, they decided to go around the back of Mccalla. They climbed over the fence and Skylar got a clip and unlocked the door. She noticed soldiers were locked in their rooms. She kept searching until she eventually found Rico's room.

Rico noticed her and told her not to touch the door. "The alarm will go off. You have to have the key." said Rico. "The doorknobs can detect prints. If it's not one of theirs it will lock the whole place down. They will have you killed and I'm not risking your life."

"Rico, I love you." said Skylar. "I feel like I have abandoned you." said Skylar.

"You haven't abandoned me." said Rico. "It's not your fault." He moved to the glass and put his hand up to meet hers.

"I want to know, are you ok?" said Skylar.

"I'm making it." said Rico. "But I'm not sure how much longer I can last. This machine is really draining me. My roommate said they are trying to completely erase our memories. They want mindless robots."

"I'm not going to let them do that." said Skylar, willing him to be strong.

All of a sudden, it sounded like one of the scientists was coming, the lights came on. Skylar and the others escaped through a laundry door that led outside.

.

One of the scientist looked into everyone's room to make sure they were still there. He saw Rico was standing up.

"Why are you not in your bed?" said Giovanni. "Were you talking to someone?"

"No, only myself." said Rico.

"Maybe, I need to check your mind again." said Giovanni. "Go to bed or I will…"

***

"We could've taken him with us." said Skylar.

"Skylar, there was no telling what we might have had to face." said Josh.

"That was a chance that I would have taken." said Skylar.

"What are you saying? That you don't need us?" said Josh. "Did we slow you down?"

"I didn't say that." said Skylar.

"What are you saying then?" said Josh.

"Josh, if you want me to, I can tell you." said Skylar. "I don't need you slowing me down."

"Both of you need to stop with this nonsense." said Levi. "I have listened to enough from the both of you. We've all been friends for a long time. Let's not ruin that now"

Mr. Bowler was in Impala setting up his next plan; the sergeant had a weapon of mass destruction so powerful that the laser could take out the world. Mr. Bowler was observing the weapon. He was amazed at how it was put together.

"Mr. Bowler, how soon will it be before you decide to take over Clark Enterprises?" said Agent Amanda.

"Soon." said Mr. Bowler

"You have everything you need to take them down." said Agent Amanda.

"You don't know the Clark family. They are a lot smarter than you think." said Mr. Bowler.

***

Skylar got out of bed early that morning. She had a nice time with her friends last night. But when she woke up she had Rico on her mind. She went outside and sat down; her hair was blowing with the wind. She bowed her head down and prayed that she would be able to figure out what to do to free Rico from Mr. Bowler. She heard a whisper in the wind.

"Skylar, you know what you must do." said her grandfather. "You are gifted with strength. Use it to save Rico and the company."

Skylar took her Mercedes Benz to quickly get to Killermike's. She went to a secret storage area in the warehouse that held more ammo then she could ever need. She grabbed the guns and bullets and called the others.

"I think I have a plan to get to Mr. Bowler" said Skylar. "Call Levi and both of you come to Killermike's."

When they arrived Skylar gave them both guns and bullets. "We are going to Mccalla and we are going to take them out."

***

Skylar's plan was to take out all of Mr. Bowler goons and get Rico and the rest of the soldiers out of there. Josh decided to throw a rock to get their attention. They were looking but didn't know where the sound was coming from. Josh and Levi got behind them and choked them from behind. There were two more guys that heard a sound and Skylar kicked up and shot and kill them both.

They went in Mccalla, with their guns pointing slightly up. Another one of Mr. Bowler's goons came out and Skylar shot him. Skylar ran down the hall to the other rooms, Josh had stolen the keys from one of the goons she shot. They released everyone from the rooms expect one door. As Skylar went to the last door, she opened it. Rico's roommate was there but not Rico.

"Where is Rico?" said Skylar.

"They took him." said the roommate.

Skylar's heart skipped a beat but she tried to keep calm. She was going to find him no matter what. She ran into the room where the scientists ran the experiments.

"Where is Rico?" said Skylar.

One of the scientists spoke up. It was Giovanni; she told her that some of Mr. Bowler goons took him away.

"Why?" said Skylar.

"I heard that Mr. Bowler is using Rico as a secret weapon." said Giovanni. "Rico is very strong. He has everything Mr. Bowler needs to take what he wants."

"You and all the other scientists need to get out of here." said Skylar.

"What are you going to do?" said Levi.

"I'm going to send Mr. Bowler a message." said Skylar.

They went into Mr. Bowler's office and took his computer and files and business information. Skylar wanted to know why Mccalla was in business.

After they loaded everything in the van, Skylar went back to Mccalla and set the building on fire. She told them all to leave.

They left before the police arrived. After several of hours Mr. Bowler got a call to say that his company was on fire.

"Who was the cause of this?" said Mr. Bowler.

"Skylar Clark." said the guy.

The guy was an ex police officer who was fired for being involved with the mob.

"She will pay dearly." said Mr. Bowler. "What better plan than to use her own boyfriend against her?" He laughed.

Rico was hooked up to the mind control machine. Mr. Bowler ordered one of his goons to send a video message to Monty's computer.

Monty was in the mansion, preparing some files for Clark Enterprises. His computer got an alert of an email from an unknown source. Monty was afraid of opening the email, he thought it might be a virus but something kept telling him to open it.

"Hi Monty. I want to tell you Bravo! Your daughter just torched my company but you know I'm looking for business elsewhere. Your father always thought he was the better man, I always hated him. I always wanted him to sell me Clark Enterprises. It was always meant to be mine."

"Since Skylar took something from me, I will take something from her." He said as he moved the camera to show Rico hooked up the mind control machine. "He will be unstoppable and there is nothing you can do about it."

Kenny came in the room; He saw the expression on Monty's face.

"I think we have a problem." said Monty. Monty let Kenny see the video message that Mr. Bowler send him by email. Kenny could not believe what he had just seen.

"Monty, what are we going to do?" said Kenny. "If we do nothing, he's coming for us and if we go to him he's prepared for us."

"We will figure this out." said Monty. "I'm going have to get in touch with my daughter and see what we can come up with."

Skylar was at Killermike's warehouse talking with Josh and Levi about Mr. Bowler and the files they had stolen from Mccalla when the phone rang.

"Skylar, we need you here as soon as possible. This is serious. Bring Josh and Levi too." said Monty

"Ok dad I'm on my way." said Skylar.

Skylar took the Mercedes she had parked at Killermike's warehouse. Josh and Levi drove their van and brought the files they had stolen from Mccalla. Monty showed them to his office.

"Looks like we have a lot on our plate." Monty said as he showed them the email.

They all saw it; Skylar couldn't bear to look at it anymore. After seeing Rico under the mind control machine she walked out of the office.

Josh decided to call all Government Agencies except for the CIA. Even though the CIA fired Agent Amanda he knew they could not be trusted. They had made no attempt to even try and find her. They needed to be kept out of this.

"The FBI, Military and Navy and all others. We will need all the help we can get" said Monty.

"While you all are doing that I'm going to check on my niece." said Kenny.

"Skylar, are you alright?" said Kenny.

"No." said Skylar. "I could have saved him."

"You will save him, Skylar." said Kenny. "I trust that you will save Clark Enterprises and Rico. I have faith in you."

"I will not lose my faith. I'll find Rico and I will save grandfather's company." said Skylar. "It's all we have left of him."

They went back into the office.

Josh and Levi looked at the files they had bought in Monty's office. They were all listed as classified. They were documents from the CIA of soldiers who were controlled by mind control. It had the name, picture and what mental state the soldiers were in.

There were even documents of soldiers back from the 1950's. The CIA experimented with a lot of brainwashing methods to control soldiers against their will. The CIA even used mind control on some of their agents.

"So we really need to come up with something." said Levi.

"I say let Mr. Bowler come to us." said Skylar. "If we go to him it may be a trap."

"I agree." said Levi. "Mr. Bowler always has a plan."

"When he comes for us, we will be ready." said Josh.

"We need to have weapons here." said Monty. "Just in case he pays us a visit. We also need cameras set up around the mansion."

"We need to make sure that nothing happens to either one of us." said Monty. "I'll be sending Ms. Rosa to her sisters so that nothing will happen to her. I wouldn't forgive myself, if something ever happened to her."

Skylar talked to her dad about Agent Amanda. "Agent Amanda is cold and heartless, but she could be under mind control without knowing?"

"It's possible." said Monty. "The only thing I know for sure is that the CIA does not play fair. They could just as easily turn on Mr. Bowler."

Chapter Five

Josh, Levi and Kenny all went out to get cameras to set up around the Clark's mansion. Skylar went out to Killermike's to bring some guns to the mansion. Monty went with Skylar to help load the guns.

As Skylar and Monty were on their way to Killermike's warehouse they heard a gunshot, a car appeared out of the blue. A guy dressed in black and white, was shooting at the car. Skylar got her gun from her belt and threw one to her father. Monty got to the back, and started shooting at the car. Skylar was flying and shooting and trying to keep the car on the highway. As they were shooting Monty managed to shoot one guy in the throat. You could see the blood rushing and then the guy on the passenger side started to shoot and was aiming at the tire. Monty was also shooting at him but missing. Skylar got him with one shot. He fell out of the car door to the highway. The last guy was the driver. When he got to Skylar he bumped the car. He was to slow at getting his gun. Monty shot him and the car ran straight into a tree, exploding into flames.

Skylar open the door to the warehouse and they both went inside. When Monty went inside, it looked like a place where you could train. One part of it had guns; it was like a shooting range and a place to do martial arts also. Monty looked on the table. There was a picture of Killermike, Skylar and Kiana.

"Your mother would have been so proud of you." said Monty.

"I know." said Skylar as she pushed the door to the ammo supply.

"Killermike had all of this?" said Monty in amazement.

"Yes." said Skylar as she grabbed all they needed to take back to the mansion.

***

Josh, Levi, and Kenny had returned back to the mansion to set up the surveillance cameras and hooked them to the computer.

Monty and Skylar came in with the weapons and Josh explained that the cameras were hidden but would send a signal to the laptop if they detected anything suspicious. Josh had loaded all of their pictures and details so it would only signal when a stranger passed by.

Skylar passed around the guns and ammo. "So now that we have the weapons, and the other government agencies on our side, the only thing we need to do now is eliminate Mr. Bowler."

"When the time comes, he will come." said Monty. "Don't let your guard down."

Mr. Bowler didn't plan on striking the mansion, but his goons had planned on it. His plan was to use Rico to get to Skylar and get her to sign over Clark Enterprises and have Rico to kill her.

After that he would begin taking on the. He wanted to be world leader with destruction and having people treat him as if he was a king.

Mr. Bowler had the mind control machine. With it he would have control over every human beings mind. They would have no control over their lives. And humanity would have no future; the world would be a dark place, with Mr. Bowler and his evilness on earth.

As long as Skylar had a single breath in her body and the willpower to destroy Mr. Bowler she would not stop until his evilness was gone for good.

Scientists were working on a plan to make Rico unstoppable, to make him follow every one of their commands and leaving him with no memory of Skylar or the Clark family.

Mr. Bowler had conducted a series of mind control tests. He had some of the scientists do tests such as checking Rico's speed and his ability in listen to the commands. They watched the movements of his body.

The tests that he conducted were the same as he used on other soldiers under mind control. Mr. Bowler had the soldiers at a mind control concentration camp.

Mr. Bowler decided to mess up all of America's frequency to all television airwaves, alerting everyone to his master invasion. But the most important of all was to end Clark Enterprises and get rid of the Clark family.

A lot of people in America were watching their television and Mr. Bowler was on every channel. Josh got a call on his cell alerting him that Mr. Bowler was television. He told Skylar and she turned the television on. They all listened.

Mr. Bowler was telling the world that he will put them under mind control. The government was already prepared to get Mr.

Bowler. They were already watching every move he made. The government had one of the scientists working for them, telling them what Mr. Bowler was up too.

Skylar told everyone, she wanted everyone training to take on this major battle. Monty stayed behind to deal with the company and to secure its accounts. The other went with Skylar to train.

Skylar tried showing Josh and Levi a little about Kajukenbo, which was a type of mixed martial arts. Kajukenbo training had a combination of striking, kicking, throwing and taking your opponent down with a little kickboxing. She showed Josh a move with kicking and landing on her feet. Josh tried and did well for the first try.

"Hey, that's not so bad." said Josh.

"Try doing it with the gun loaded." said Skylar.

"I don't know about that." said Josh.

"Come on, Josh." said Levi.

So, Josh tried to catch the gun without shooting himself.

"Levi you're next." said Skylar. Skylar handed Levi the gun as he flipped catching the gun and landing on his feet.

"You both are doing great." said Skylar.

Skylar had them do something else. She had them point the gun at an object, hitting it straight from a distance. They both shot and hit it right in the centre.

"I think you're ready." said Skylar.

"I'm ready." said Levi.

Josh told Skylar he was going to head back out, to find out if there was any more information about Mr. Bowler. Levi headed out with him.

Josh and Levi were in the van, Josh was driving when all of a sudden Josh got a call about Agent Amanda. She was back in America; Mr. Bowler was not with her.

It seemed like she was making plans of her own. Agent Amanda was going to Clark Enterprises, to kill Monty Clark and that she had some of Mr. Bowler goons with her.

Monty was sitting at his desk with client accounts and paperwork with his cup of coffee.

Agent Amanda had disguised herself as a delivery woman delivering a package to get in Clark Enterprises. Agent Amanda had accessed the Clark Enterprise's computer and found a client file. She put the client name on the package to make it seem real.

Agent Amanda had her long hair pulled back into a bun, and a hat with Ups on the front, with a brown Ups shirt and dark blue dress pants.

The goons were hidden, so that the security opened the door. Agent Amanda shot the security very quick with a gun that was very silent, you couldn't hear the shot. She took the security keys and access card. Agent Amanda opened the door for the goons to come in Clark Enterprises.

"Alright guys come in." said Agent Amanda.

As agent Amanda was letting them in, she didn't see anyone around. But one of the Clark Enterprises employees saw her; she was taking a bathroom break.

The lady took off her heels, so that Agent Amanda and her goon couldn't hear her as she quickly ran down the hall. She went directly to Monty's door, slowly closing it and locking the door.

"Why are you in my office?" Monty demanded to know. "What's going on out there?"

She told him what she had seen. Monty went into his desk and loaded his gun. He went to his computer security system to send an alert that would warn the police and the other employees.

"This doesn't seem right." said the goon. "The Clarks wouldn't let you in that easily. It's too quiet"

"Maybe they are working." said Agent Amanda

"Who in the hell made you a CIA agent?" said one of the goons. "We should have stayed behind."

"Mr. Bowler would have us killed for disobeying his orders." said the other goon as he had his gun in the air, looking around to see if Monty was around.

Suddenly there was a gunshot and he went down. Monty had shot the goon in the back.

Josh and Levi called Skylar and told her what was going down, that Agent Amanda had a planned to kill her father at Clark Enterprises.

When Monty shot the goon, he had to hide so the rest of them couldn't see him.

At the same time, he was trying to protect his employee. Her name was Trinity. He told her to be quiet, that help would be along soon.

Agent Amanda and the rest of the goons didn't know where the shots were coming from. Clark Enterprises was a huge building, the goons and Agent Amanda separated.

Skylar drove very fast to get to Clark Enterprises. She met Josh and Levi at the entrance.

The Security System did a facial recognition. It matched Skylar's face to the Clark's family database.

She called Kenny and told him to come immediately. She turned to the others.

"I need you to make sure no one comes to the mansion." said Skylar. "Get the guns loaded."

As, Skylar, josh and Levi walked slowly with their guns, it was very quiet as they went down the hall, they noticed that one of the goons was dead the hallway.

"Dad must have had shot him."

They looked through the door and went down a little further down the hall. They heard footsteps. The goons spotted them and start shooting. Skylar ran behind them. She flipped up and dropped behind them, and shot them.

The two goons went down; the other two were chasing Josh and Levi. Josh shot one of them right in the heart. Levi shot the other one right in the head.

Monty and Trinity were in the Clark Enterprises basement. They were hiding from Agent Amanda.

"Monty. I know you're here, I just want to talk to you." said Agent Amanda.

Monty loaded his gun, stepped out and pointed it straight at her.

"Now which one of us you think will die first?" said Agent Amanda.

"It's not going to be me." said Monty.

"I will make Mr. Bowler very proud." said Agent Amanda.

"Tell me this Agent Amanda, what are you getting out of all of this?" said Monty. "Do really think Mr. Bowler is going to be happy that you did this without him?"

"I don't care what you say. He's a fool." said Agent Amanda. "I did everything I could for him and all he wanted was this stupid company. I figure if I killed you then Mr. Bowler will finally appreciate me."

Before she knew it, Skylar came from behind her and kicked her. Agent Amanda fell over and lost her gun. She tried to reach for the gun but Skylar grabbed her. She punched Skylar. Skylar head-butted her. Skylar was getting the best of Agent Amanda but she still managed to grab the gun. She jumped to her feet and pointed it at Skylar.

Monty came quickly from behind and shot her in the back of the head. She fell.

Josh and Levi came down to the basement. They saw that Agent Amanda was dead.

"Alright!" Skylar said to Josh.

"Who is the lady? said Levi while pointing towards Trinity.

"She is the one that alerted us to all of this. Make sure she gets home safely." said Monty.

"So do you think Mr. Bowler has anyone else out to kill you?" said Skylar.

"No, this was not a part of his plan." said Monty. "It was all Agent Amanda. She wanted Mr. Bowler to appreciate her for killing me. I believe she was in love with Mr. Bowler. He doesn't love anyone, not even himself."

"How could she love someone like him?" said Skylar.

"Some people just have a twisted way of loving someone." said Monty.

"I'm getting ready to go back to the mansion." said Skylar.

"I'll let Kenny know you're alright." said Skylar.

Chapter Six

Back at Impala Mr. Bowler had learned of what happened. He had his scientists create a frequency way through satellite to hear the Clark family conversations. Mr. Bowler was furious, about what she had done but that wasn't going to stop his plan.

Agent Amanda was in love with Mr. Bowler but as far as he was concerned she was just another failure.

***

Skylar got to the mansion to check on Kenny. He had his gun ready. He heard someone pull in and he checked out the surveillance camera to see actually who it was.

"Skylar! Is Monty OK?"

"Yes he's fine." said Skylar. "Agent Amanda is dead. I just came to make sure you were alright. I'm going back to Clark Enterprises now."

"I'm coming with you." said Kenny.

***

Clark Enterprises was surrounded by CIA agents and police cars. There was yellow tape around the building warning people not to step inside. Skylar asked for Monty and one of the policemen told her he was inside talking to the chief.

"It looks like you and your family continue to be a target." said the chief. "Start from the beginning, what happened?"

Monty told him everything.

"You have the entire force on your side." said the chief of police. "We will find him."

He looked at Agent Amanda's body. The medical examiner was preparing to move her when someone stopped him.

"Who are you?" said the chief of police.

My name is Agent Gary Fallon, I'm from the CIA. Agent Amanda belongs to the CIA even though she betrayed us."

"Well this Agent, or ex agent of yours tried to kill Mr. Monty Clark." said the chief of police. "The medical examiner needs to investigate this. I've heard about you guys at the CIA"

"What have you heard?" said Agent Fallon.

"What you do to people." said the chief of police.

"That's nothing but hearsay." said Agent Fallon. "I'm not interested in that. I'm here with the rest of the agents from the CIA to take Agent Amanda back."

"Is there something you're trying to hide?" said the chief of police.

"No, not at all." said Agent Fallon.

Monty stepped in and advised him to let her go. They didn't need any more trouble right now.

Skylar and Kenny came in.

"What are you doing?" Skylar asked.

"It seems like the CIA doesn't want Agent Amanda to go to the medical examiner here in Lance County." said Monty.

"Don't give them the body." said Skylar.

"We said that…" the chief of police. "But keeping her here would be a federal offense."

"Dad, we are so close." said Skylar. "The medical examiner could have checked Agent Amanda to see if there was some of the mind control in her system."

"They are up to something." said Monty.

The other CIA agents took the body and put it in the van.

"They're not fooling anyone. Agent Amanda is a cover up." said Kenny. "They don't want people to know just exactly what the CIA is up too."

Monty told them all to go to his office while he spoke to the chief. "Do you think you could get on my computer and find out about this special Agent Fallon?"

The Chief of police told Monty he had someone who could hack the system.

The guy's name was Jeffery Kizer. He was in prison for hacking government agency databases and releasing information to other countries. He was given life in prison.

The police asked him to come to Monty's office.

The chief of police told Jeffery "I know you're wondering why I brought you here. I want to make a deal with you. I can get you a reduced sentence if you hack the CIA's system for us."

Jeffery went over to the computer and accessed the CIA government site and went into the database.

"What exactly are you looking for?" said Jeffery.

"We are looking for Agent Fallon."

Jeffery put his name into the CIA database. It showed a picture of him. It said he was an agent since 1992. He was a respected agent with special orders to clean out agents who were trying to expose the CIA.

"So basically, he's the CIA's little puppet." said Kenny.

"Basically." said Jeffery.

"Does it say anything else about Agent Fallon?" said the chief of police.

"No, nothing." said Jeffery.

"Try Agent Amanda." said Kenny.

Agent Amanda had been an Agent for the CIA since 1998. She had been under mind control. All of her files were marked as classified.

"I knew that they were hiding something." said the chief of police.

"The mind control drug can be found in the bloodstream. It shows as moving particles." said Jeffery.

"So is the CIA working with Mr. Bowler?" Kenny asked.

Jeffery looked into the database to figure out if Mr. Bowler and the CIA were working together. He found a set of files that were listed as confidential.

In the file there were pictures of Mr. Bowler shaking hands with Agent Fallon and picture of the mind control machine and the drugs that went with it.

"It looks like you got your answers." said Jeffery.

"We will have to find Agent Fallon." said Skylar. "If he is supplying Mr. Bowler with agents then he needs to be taken down first."

They all agreed to help each other to take him out. They could not do it alone. This required team work.

Skylar and Kenny went back to the mansion. Skylar still couldn't shake the feeling that she hadn't done enough to help Rico. Even if she did find him she knew he would not be the same man she fell in love with.

She knew there could be a chance that she might have to kill the man she loved. But she wanted to be with Rico for the rest of her life.

***

Mr. Bowler had made a visit to the headquarters of the CIA. He was there to visit Agent Fallon. He approached the security desk demanding to see Agent Fallon.

"Do you have an appointment?" said the secretary.

"No, but he's just dying to see me." said Mr. Bowler.

She got on the phone and made a call to Agent Fallon. He told her to send Mr. Bowler in.

"Have a seat." said Agent Bowler.

"Good job getting Agent Amanda body away from the police." said Mr. Bowler.

"I do as instructed and as I'm paid to do." said Agent Fallon.

"I want you to keep a sharp eye on the Clark family." said Mr. Bowler. "Taking Agent Amanda away from the medical examiner has raised suspicions. Never underestimate the Clark family."

"Never underestimate me." said Agent Fallon. "There is nothing the Clark's can do to me."

"That's what Agent Amanda thought." said Mr. Bowler.

"Agent Amanda never deserved to be a CIA agent." said Agent Fallon. "If they come for me, I'll be ready."

***

Back at the mansion Skylar picked up her phone and called Josh.

"Josh do you think, you can contact someone who knows about the CIA? Someone who can help us get rid of Agent Fallon?"

"I might be able to find someone." said Josh. "The ex CIA agent I know has been in hiding for many years. He would be taking a huge risk that could leave him exposed. The CIA threatened to kill him years ago because he tried to bring down the rogue agents. He had to change his identity. His name is Jack Nelson now. I'll work quickly to find him."

Josh drove to a nearby bar. He knew Jack spent time there. When he went inside the bar he saw Jack. He was disguised as an older man leaning over a drink. Josh sat beside him and told him what he needed from him.

He told Josh that he had been reading the papers. He already had an idea that Bowler was working with the CIA.

He felt that the Clark family didn't deserve what they were going through. And what they were about to face was only the beginning. He wanted to help the Clark family end Agent Fallon.

He decided to go with Josh to go see Skylar at the Clark's mansion.

Jack knew that some of the agents had secrets. He knew them better than they knew themselves.

As Josh was driving he called Skylar and told her to get everyone together and meet him at the mansion.

They went inside and sat down. The others were eager to hear Jake's suggestions.

Jake knew some of the spots that Agent Fallon hung out. He said that sometimes Agent Fallon would eat his lunch at Forest Hill Park. He cut all of his CIA gadgets off and left them at the headquarters. That was one way to kill him.

He also told them that he liked to party at Club 909. That would be another place to catch him off guard.

"He knows who we are but he doesn't know who you are in disguise." said Skylar.

"I'll go the club in disguise." said Jake. "You guys will be in your cars watching my back."

So that was the decision they had made to go after Agent Fallon when he least expected.

They ate dinner together and then prepared themselves for what they were going to face. Skylar got her 9mm and Glock 27 and placed them in her belt.

Jake rode with Skylar to club 909. When they arrived Agent Fallon was going in. Jake followed him quietly.

There were lots of people dancing and drinking. There were two women right beside Agent Fallon and he was buying drinks and flashing them money.

Jake sat down at a table in the club and ordered a drink. He sat there watching, Agent Fallon for hours.

Finally people started leaving. The bartender refused to give Agent Fallon anymore to drink so he left.

It was dark but the outside lights were on. Jake went behind him.

As he was about to kill agent Fallon he turned and around and pulled his gun on him.

"You think I don't know who you are in that disguise?" said Agent Fallon. "I've wanted to find you for years. You're Agent Jake Nelson, you're a disgrace to the CIA."

All of a sudden he heard a sound and car lights came on. The headlights blinded him and he shot towards one of the cars.

Jake jumped on his back, and he got him down on the ground. Skylar got out of the car, jumped up and did a kick and knocked him down. He tried to get back up but Skylar got him with one shot to the head.

They rushed back to the mansion; they knew it wouldn't be long before the CIA got word about Agent Fallon. They needed to figure out a plan to get Jake out of Lance County. It was time for Jake to create a new identity.

As they got to the mansion, Jake took of his disguise. He disguised himself as someone completely different. He dyed his hair and gave himself a close shave. He even changed his eye color with contact lenses.

Josh helped him get the identification cards and passport for a whole new life. Skylar ordered the plane tickets and gave him a couple of thousands to help him out a little with his new life.

***

Mr. Bowler tried to call Agent Fallon the next day. There were no answer so he sent one of his goons to find out what was going on. He had a hunch that Agent Fallon was dead after he warned him about the Clark family. He didn't listen. He was just another person that failed him.

***

Police and the CIA, were on the scene at Club 909. The CIA took the investigation over; once they found out he was one of their own.

One of his goons took a cell phone picture of the scene and sent it to Mr. Bowler.

"What happened?" said Mr. Bowler.

"He was killed at the Club 909." said the goon.

"Do they know who did it?" said Mr. Bowler.

"The police are investigating, but the CIA took it over." said the goon.

"If the Clark's didn't do it, it must be one of their own." said Mr. Bowler. "The CIA will not share that secret. My plan is ruined. I guess I have to resort to plan B."

"What is plan B boss?" said one of the goons.

"Agent Fallon was our supplier." said Mr. Bowler. "The CIA is still working with us, but they are being investigated by the government. We have enough of the mind control drugs and machine to have everything go as planned. We will use what we have."

"I can get the scientists to remake a fresh batch of the mind control." said Mr. Bowler.

Just as Mr. Bowler stated, the CIA were in hot water with the government. The news about the CIA spread all around the globe.

People started to feel that they had lost their faith in the government. Everyone at Clark Enterprises were sitting down and watching the news.

"Mr. Bowler is taking full control over his sick plan." said Levi.

"We need to have more info on Mr. Bowler." said Monty.

"We still have Giovanni." said Josh. "She can tell us about Mr. Bowler and maybe figure out a way to stop the soldiers."

"It might be a shot." said Monty.

"If we can get in contact with Giovanni maybe she can help us create a larger quality of X-steno that we will let out as a gas, it will reverse the mind control." said Skylar.

"Skylar, you are brilliant." said Josh. "So when they bust into Clark Enterprises we will set off the gas and Mr. Bowler's plan will be destroyed."

"Mr. Bowler will never stop going after my grandfather's company." said Skylar. "I will never let his crooked hands on it. Even if it kills me."

"Skylar, this is not only your fight. It's all of ours." said Levi.

"Yeah, we are a team." said Josh. He went to his computer to find out the exact location where Giovanni was hiding out. He called her phone.

"Giovanni, we might need your help." said Josh.

"Josh, you know if Mr. Bowler finds out he will kill me." said Giovanni. "What do you need me to do for you?"

"We want you to make a gas out of the x-steno mind reverse drug." said Josh.

"That's a brilliant idea." said Giovanni. "Ok, I'll do it. Meet me, at the old house towards the alley down town."

Josh went to meet her. He had the X-steno with him. It was just a sample but it was enough for her to make a grenade full that would reverse the mind control in seconds.

Josh went back to tell Skylar that everything was set.

"So when Mr. Bowler decides to come we will be ready for him." said Josh. "We have the other government agencies on our side now too."

"I'm just wondering if he has all of these soldiers, why does he need Rico?" said Skylar.

"He wants to get under your skin." said Josh. "If it comes to the point then you have to kill Rico. Skylar, I'm sorry to say this but you will have to do it."

"If I have to I will." said Skylar.

***

Mr. Bowler had the soldiers in shackles as they slept. They were just prisoners to him and he refused to show them any kindness or comfort.

One of the guards shoved one of the soldiers on the ground for no apparently reason. Rico jumped up and tried to fight the guard. Rico had the guard down and stumped him but it only resulted in the rest of them attacking him.

As they were hitting Rico he started to experience a sudden flashback of people that he knew. Little bits were coming back to him. Skylar. Her friends and family.

He lay on the ground, his nose swollen with blood. One of the guards spoke up and told them to stop. Mr. Bowler needed him to carry out his plans. They pulled him off the ground and sent him back to his cell.

As Rico lay down on the hard, uncomfortable bed he tried to figure out who this woman was that was appearing before him. Seeing her made him feel happy. He drifted into a deep sleep.

The memories kept coming. He saw that the woman that he was dreaming about wasn't an ordinary woman. The woman had advanced training in martial arts and gun training. He couldn't figure out why he was dreaming about this woman. What was the connection?

Finally, it hit him all at once, his heart started to beat fast, he remembered who she was. She was the woman he wanted to spend his life with. The images were there but they were fading. The mind control was slowly wiping them away.

He looked over to the side of the bed. He picked up a rock and carved Skylar's name on the wall. He figured if he could look at her name he would never forget her.

A guy from the other cell started to talk to him.

"I heard what you did for that guy. Good move on your part."

"Who are you?" said Rico.

"My name is West." he said.

"I also did the same as you. I couldn't bear to see the guards beating up someone." said West as he offered Rico a cigarette through the bars.

"Do you think we have any chance of getting out of here?" said Rico.

"No." said West. "Trust me, I want to but we will need a lot of backup. With the security around here they will spot us and kill us right on the spot. We have to tough it out."

"You're right." said Rico. "I have faith that I will get out of here, and once I'm clear from the mind control I will ask the women I want to share my life with to marry me."

"That's a huge commitment." said West.

"Do you have any memories of having any relationships?" said Rico.

"I remember being married." said West. "I feel that god will help me, lead me back to my soul mate."

"I feel the same way." said Rico.

"Son, what's her name?" said West.

"Skylar." said Rico.

"Skylar, that name sounds familiar." said West. "Is she the one that owns that billion dollar company that Mr. Bowler wants so badly?"

"Yes!" said Rico.

"So when Mr. Bowler sends us, this Skylar is going to be waiting for him." said West.

"She will not give up without a fight." said Rico. "My girlfriend is trained in martial arts and gun shooting. She shoots faster than you can blink."

"Even though she can do all of this, what you are going in a state of mind control." said West.

"You're the master plan to all of this." said West.

"What do you mean?" said Rico.

"Mr. Bowler plans on using you to kill Skylar." said west.

"That can't happen." said Rico.

"Rico, what you will have to do is fight the mind control. You have to fight it in order for you to save Skylar." said West.

They heard footsteps. It was the guards coming back. He quickly gave West his lighter back. He made sure the cigarette disappeared. They both pretended to sleep.

The guard unlocked the door. Mr. Bowlers was just behind him. He had come to see Rico.

"I see you haven't been doing too good Rico." said Mr. Bowler. Let's cut to the chase. Do you have any memories of anything? Has anything come back to you?"

"No." said Rico.

"Do you know the name Skylar?" said Mr. Bowler.

"No." said Rico

"We have a battle to face against Clark Enterprises. I need you to listen to my every command." said Mr. Bowler.

"I will." said Rico.

"Get some rest." said Mr. Bowler.

He turned to the guard and whispered to him to tell the scientist to inject Rico again. Just to make sure he was still under the mind control.

The scientists came to inject him with the drug and all of a sudden his memories that had come back to him were completely gone again.

**

Skylar was a Killermike's. She prayed that her family would make it through this alive.

The time had come for the fight of her life. She tried to clear Rico out of her mind as she trained. Rico was under Mr. Bowler's mind control and she knew she had to face him.

Josh informed the president about the mind control drug antidote that was formed into a grenade to help reverse the mind control.

Josh called Monty and asked where Skylar was.

"She's at Killermike's." said Monty.

Josh told Monty and Kenny to get to Clark Enterprises. The battle was about to start. He called Skylar too and told her to get back to the mansion.

At Clark Enterprises everyone was armed with weapons to face Mr. Bowler and his soldiers.

Mr. Bowler and Rico were on a helicopter. The soldiers flew in on planes.

All of the sudden there was a big sound. The helicopter flew into Clark Enterprises. Rico and Mr. Bowler appeared form the smoke.

Rico started shooting and shots were fired back at him.

A plane from the government threw a grenade filled with the mind control antidote.

Some of them were not hit by the antidote; Monty and Kenny were shooting and fighting. Josh and Levi were shooting at Rico. Rico was shooting back at them.

Mr. Bowler and Skylar were fighting and shooting at each other.

Finally, Rico had shot Josh in the arm.

Josh hid behind the file cabin as blood rushed from his arm. Levi kept shooting. Skylar saw that Josh was hit.

Mr. Bowler had taken off. She went after him.

Rico came after her, she turned around with a kick and punch to Rico's face.

Levi shot Mr. Bowler and hit him in the shoulder. Mr. Bowler shouted in pain and shot Levi. The bullet went straight through his heart.

Mr. Bowler went to get his helicopter to get his mass destruction weapon out to blow the Clark's family away.

As Skylar was fighting with Rico, she remembered she had the x-steno drug in her belt in a syringe to inject Rico. She got Rico down and injected him. He didn't move. Then he slowly opened his eyes and got up.

Rico jumped and pulled her out of the way of Mr. Bowler's mass destruction machine.

Monty told Kenny to go one way and he would find another way to get the machine away from Mr. Bowler.

As they were planning Skylar appeared and shot Mr. Bowler in the head.

The mass destruction machine was about to fall but Rico caught it and stopped it.

The police came and took away the machine.

Skylar was upset. Levi was a dear friend and he was dead.

Skylar gave Rico a hug and kiss.

Rico asked Skylar if she would marry him. She said yes.

"It's finally over." said Kenny.

"It's over." said Monty.

"I guess we're ready for a wedding." said Kenny.

"Rico, welcome to the family." said Monty.

****

Stay tuned for Smooth Intentions 3 - Ghostly Realm.

Check out the Smooth Intentions series from the beginning.

Some wonderful reviews it has received.

5.0 out of 5 stars! I love lots of action…especially in a book!!!

By J. Summers on October 27, 2014

Format: Kindle Edition

If this really is Kimberly Stewart's first book then…WOW!!! I can't wait to see what's to come. This book was awesome! It's entertaining, exciting, and have characters that will leave you yearning for more! If you're looking for a book to take you on an exhilarating ride, this is it!

About Author Kimberly Stewart

Kimberly Stewart is a mother, author and songwriter. She is also a fashion student at Academy of Arts pursuing a bachelor's degree in fashion design.

Stay tuned for more books. To come soon - Dangerous love, House Unknown and many more.